BEYOND THE GATE

A Bindarra Creek Mystery Romance

RHONDA FORREST

Valeena Press

For the wonderful neighbours
I've been lucky enough
to always have.

Chapter 1

Charlotte peered through the car windscreen at the blinding winter rain. Window wipers, working furiously, did little to push back the tide of water that flowed over the glass. She stopped at an intersection, checking the road signs as she drove through the middle of the small town of Bindarra Creek. The street was deserted, only a few dim lights glowing outside the closed shops and businesses on the main street. Cars parked outside the Riverside Pub stood in a torrent of water that gushed down the side of the street. Large puddles covered sections of the bitumen and she avoided them, hoping like crazy the roads she needed to travel on would not be flooded.

When she came to the T-intersection she turned left; the dim lights of the Cyprus Café letting her know she was on the right street. Winding her way around she slowed again, checking her bearings and the directions she'd been given. The R.S.L. club and the public hospital appeared on her right and a sign, Mt Ingalls Road, was just visible through the rain. Picking up speed she followed the road that would lead her out of town. The road narrowed as she cleared the outskirts of the town and eventually, she came to what she was looking for: a wooden road sign, "Forrest Road" directed her to turn right. Charlotte indicated and turned the car, slowing once again as bitumen turned into dirt. Tall trees and thick bush lined the side of the road and large branches waved wildly in the howling wind. Twigs and lumps of bark flew through the air and she flinched at the sound of them hitting the car. What a night to be driving, especially on these back roads she didn't know well. Thank goodness—from what she remembered— the property wasn't too much further.

The bush soon cleared to open paddocks and the entire landscape lit up as a flash of white light split the sky. Rolling hills dotted with trees and large boulders were visible for a second and Charlotte took a deep breath, relieved her destination was nearby and she'd soon be safe and away from this awful storm. Another jagged bolt of lightning and a loud clap of thunder made her jump. She looked ahead; a large metal gate blocked her from driving any further. Annoyed, she pulled up and turned the engine off, the headlights lighting up the gate blocking her entrance.

The last thing she wanted to do was get out in the pouring rain, but there was no use just sitting here dry and warm, hoping the gate would somehow magically open. The rain showed no sign of abating, so with a sigh, Charlotte grabbed her torch and got out of the car. Stepping carefully over the puddles, she tried to avoid the deeper holes, but the muddy water soon covered her shoes and soaked the bottom of her jeans. Water streamed down her face, drenching her from head to toe and she tucked her head down low trying to protect herself from the icy wind. She gritted her teeth, her hands shaking as she wrapped her scarf tighter around her shoulders.

The light from her torch shone on the gate and she expelled her breath in frustration. A heavy chain fastened with a padlock was wrapped around a thick wooden post. Shaking the gate, she swore loudly when it didn't budge. The entry to the property she had just purchased was through a shared easement between her place, and the exclusive polo establishment, Bentley Estate, next door. Hunter Sullivan, the real estate guy, had told her that the gate was never locked, and both properties used it without any drama. There hadn't been a padlock on the gate when she'd inspected the estate. The only keys she'd been given were to the house, sheds, and other buildings on the property. Another loud clap of thunder rumbled across the sky and a bolt of lightning lit up the paddocks in front of her. Her hands clenched into fists as the rain lashed across her face, her body shaking from frustration as well as the cold.

Racing back to the car she cursed Hunter. Surely the neighbours knew she was arriving today? Bindarra Creek was a small township and the fact that an outsider had bought the sprawling farm on Forrest Road and was turning it into a writers and artists' retreat, would no doubt have the townsfolk—and her neighbours —talking.

Her hands shook as she pushed the button for Hunter's after-hours number. *Please*, she pleaded silently, *please let there be phone reception.*

"Thank goodness," she shouted down the phone when he answered. Another loud clap of thunder rent the air and the trees at the side of the road flung their leaves and small branches onto the bonnet of her car.

"Charlotte here. Charlotte Dawson. I'm at the gate, but there's a lock on it." Her voice shook as she tried to stop her teeth chattering.

Hunter's deep voice was a welcome sound. "Charlotte? I thought you were moving in this morning?"

"I was supposed to, but I was held up. But I'm here now, standing at the gate. It's locked. I can't get in."

"What! That gate's never locked. Hell Charlotte, there's a doozy of a storm here at the moment. Is your brother with you?"

"No. That was the holdup today. It's a long story and I'll fill you in another time. All I want to do is to get into the house. Now. I'm drenched."

Hunter paused. "I'm looking after the twins. My wife's at a meeting so I can't come and help you out. I tell you what though, I'll give Alex next door to you a call. I'm pretty sure he's home tonight. They must have put a lock on that gate for some reason. Stay there. I'll ring you back."

The car swayed a little as the wind picked up. What a typical end to an awful day. Jacob, her older brother, was supposed to be helping her move in. He'd been going to stay for the week and make sure she got settled, but he'd rung this morning.

"I feel dreadful and I never usually let you down, but…."

Charlotte hated *buts*. Someone had once told her that in a sentence, everything that came before *but* could be disregarded.

And it was true.

Jacob had been upset. "You know I'd do anything

4

for you, sis. I'm trying my best to free up the time, *but* Cecilia is threatening to pack her bags. She's only been back a week and now she's leaving again. She says it's over. I need time to talk to her and make her realise she can't do this again. You were right when you said I was being too nice. I shouldn't have let her back although this time I know I don't have feelings for her anymore, so maybe it's been for the best. I'm sorry, I can't make it. You'll be okay, and I'll get down there as soon as I can. I just need some time to sort this mess out."

Her phone dinged and Charlotte looked down, reading the message from Hunter.

Alex is on his way. He said the gate isn't locked. Message me when you get in.

Hopefully, this morning and tonight weren't an indication of what was to come. This move to Bindarra Creek was going to fulfil her dream. As well as—she scrunched up her face, looking at the water pouring over the car—as well as giving her something to concentrate on after her marriage breakup.

Twenty-five to thirty-five. Ten years she felt like she'd tipped down the drain, flushed down the toilet. Ten years of a husband trying to convince her what he wanted was important in life. Ten years of arguing in her mind that she wasn't being true to herself.

Now, there would be no more wasting time. She knew what was important in life and she wasn't going to smile and put up with what she didn't agree with anymore. Those days were over, as were romance, men, and definitely marriage. A lesson had been learned. If only she hadn't been so stubborn and instead listened to her family, as well as Aunt Lucille about getting married so young. Men could not be trusted. It might appear they loved you, worshipped the ground you stood on, bought you expensive jewellery, and held you like you were the most important person in the world. The trouble was that they were all weasels—sneaky, conniving, two-timing mongrels who lied through their teeth and thought they were God's gift to women.

Charlotte gripped the steering wheel, her knuckles white.

Let go. Let go of the steering wheel.

She closed her eyes.

Don't let the fury rise.

A new life beckoned. Away from the city, away from the glitter strip of the Gold Coast, and all that pretentious stuff she'd never wanted anyway. The bimbo could have it all, and the bimbo could have Hugh.

Thank goodness the inheritance from Aunty Lucille had come through after the divorce and not before. Her stomach rolled as she thought of how horrendous it would have been if, Hugh, who stated his profession as 'developer', had got his hands on it. There would have been some get-rich-quick plan that he would have wanted to invest in, a business idea that was going to make a million dollars. The inheritance would have gone in the blink of an eye, down the same road her own savings had gone. It would add to the list of, "you just got a give it time, babe, these things aren't quick money-making plans, they're major investments, you have to be patient."

No, this money had bought her dream, Forrest Glen.

Nothing would stop her from doing what she wanted now she was her own person. If she kept telling herself that, it would happen. Don't let anything or anyone get in your way. Not even a big fat padlock on a gate that wasn't supposed to be locked.

Headlights coming towards her from the other side of the gate broke her reverie.

"At last," she murmured.

A man dressed in a long waterproof coat climbed out of the car, a large umbrella shielding him from the heavy rain. He tried to open the gate, shaking it as she had, before returning to his car. Someone in the passenger's seat passed him something and she watched as the man walked back to the padlocked gate. He unlocked the padlock and swung the gate wide open.

Charlotte breathed a sigh of relief. The storm showed no sign of weakening and all she wanted was a hot shower and dry clothes. She wound the window down a little as the man came to the side of her car. He shouted over the sound of the storm.

"G'day. I'm Alex Bentley from next door. That padlock's never locked. It just hangs there, has done for years. I'm not sure what's happened. Maybe some kids snapped it shut. Anyway, I'll take it off. Hunter rang to let me know you were locked out."

"Charlotte. My name's Charlotte. Thank you."

He waved her through as she called out to him. "Thank you, again."

Chapter 2

The weather did not improve. The rain became heavier and the wind continued to howl as Charlotte drove the short distance to the house. A narrow concrete path led to the front verandah and she parked as close as she could to the front steps. There was no covered area to park under and for a while, she contemplated sleeping in the car. Draping her arms over the steering wheel she closed her eyes, her energy sapped from the long drive and a week of packing and organising before she'd left. The noise of the rain on the car was deafening and she questioned if she had the energy to get out and bring her bags in. Sitting up she pressed her face to the side window, rivers of rain pouring down its surface. Aunt Lucille would have said to get out and get moving.

It's only water, it won't kill you.

Taking a deep breath, she grabbed what she needed, opened the car door and made a dash for the front steps. Thankfully the front door was unlocked and the verandah offered some protection from the rain. By the time she managed to drag a couple of bags, her sleeping bag and camp mattress into the house, she felt like a drowned rat. At least the electricity worked, the toilet flushed and although the hot water system was turned off, she told herself that in the morning the water should be warm enough for a shower. The large fireplace beckoned but there was no hope of that tonight. A spot on the lounge floor would have to do. A dry-off with a towel and a change into fresh clothes left her feeling slightly better and she curled up on her mattress. Her sleeping bag and a blanket kept her warm and she snuggled in, the dramas of the long day sending her into a heavy sleep.

THE OVERGROWN TWENTY-HECTARE PROPERTY, situated at the end of Forrest Road, had literally popped out at Charlotte from the real estate pages she spent half her life perusing now she didn't have any other aim in life. The previous year had been a rollercoaster of ups and downs, the routines of ten years of marriage thrown into chaos as she tried to get over her divorce with Hugh. She'd continued her teaching job when they separated. It had given her something to focus on and stopped her thinking about him and the bimbo. While she was busy with her year one class, she didn't have time to worry about how she'd been made a fool of, or think about the lies that she'd swallowed.

With a class of twenty-five five-year-olds, she hadn't been afforded a spare second of downtime. Continuing in her job and not taking time off to drown in her sorrows and anger had been the best decision she'd made for a long time. Jacob had offered for her to live with him and his girlfriend, Cecilia. That wasn't exactly the ideal situation either, as Jacob and Cecilia had an on-off, then on-again relationship that never ran smoothly. He needed to end the romance, or "convenience", as her father liked to refer to it and get on with his life. Then again, who was she to be giving advice?

I can't even manage my own affairs.

So, with nowhere else to go, she'd packed what she needed and moved in with Jacob. Thankfully she had spent most of the time in her bedroom, using the excuse that she was getting lessons ready and trying to work out what she was going to do with her life. She needed time to herself to get her thoughts in order.

Jacob lived on Tamborine Mountain in the Gold Coast Hinterland, the perfect place to retreat to, away from anything that was associated with her old life and Hugh. Charlotte knew she needed a massive change, a move away from people who she never wanted to see ever again. Most of the people she'd socialised with were Hugh's friends anyway. She'd kept her friends at work separate from her home life, the chance of a coffee with a group of them after work had provided a calm, fun time compared to the intensity of time spent with Hugh. Apart from her family, who she knew would visit her wherever she lived, there was really nothing keeping her at the Gold Coast. Although she loved teaching, she also decided that it was time for a career change. A new challenge to distract her from wallowing over the past, wasted years.

"But you've only been teaching for seven years," her mum said, horrified that her only daughter would consider a professional change this early in life. "I thought you'd stay in teaching until you had a family of your own."

"Well, Mum, not everything goes as planned, and thank goodness I didn't have kids with Hugh, otherwise, I'd have to share them with him and the bimbo. That would be something else I'd have to contend with. At least this is clean-cut. There is nothing that ties me to him."

"Doesn't sound like you got any money from him," her father added.

Her tone lightened when she spoke to her father. He was a sweetheart and like Mum, all he wanted was for her to be happy.

"No, Dad. I didn't. He wasted the lot and our mortgage was up to the hilt. He's sold that stupid fancy house that I never wanted, the flash cars and expensive furniture. You know those things don't matter to me. I can't believe I went along with it for so long. He was never like that at the start. I wish you'd said more over the last few years."

"We know, love," Dad had said. "Hugh changed when he took on that new job and began mixing with all the highflyers. I could see the edge of it there with him at the start but I thought you'd keep him level-headed. It was hard for your mother and me to say anything. We did try though."

"Thanks, Dad. I know. This is my fault and no one else's. I have nothing to my name but at least I'm not in debt. The loans are paid out and I guess I'll just start again."

"We love you, darling," her mother added. "Anything you need, we're here for you."

"Thanks, Mum. You know I'd ask if I needed. I can

stay with Jacob until I work out what I want to do. I'm also going to visit Aunt Lucille during the next round of school holidays. I've been in contact with her and she's excited I'm coming. Perhaps I'll end up in Sydney. There are plenty of jobs down there and it would be a fresh new start."

Aunt Lucille, her mother's older sister, lived surrounded by her small dog, beloved cats and paintings, on the harbour in Sydney. Her husband had died many years ago and she'd always told Charlotte and Jacob that their Uncle Bernard had been the love of her life and she'd never find anyone as good as him again. She never remarried and with no family of her own, Charlotte and Jacob were the closest thing to having her own children. Charlotte's dad always said that Lucille was wildly eccentric and in a world of her own. She was, however, the best aunt any child could wish for and her house was a fabulous place to offload kids to in the school holidays.

Unlike home, when you were on holiday with Aunt Lucille, there were hardly any boundaries or rules. The main ones were that you were only allowed within a five-mile radius, no train travel, no getting in cars or talking to strangers, and to be home by dark. "The world, or Sydney, is your oyster," Aunt Lucille told them.

They didn't have a clue how far five miles was. It didn't matter though, there was plenty to keep them occupied close by, the gardens as well as the beautiful Sydney Harbour providing an idyllic playground.

Aunt Lucille had passed away not long after Charlotte had left Hugh.

Her gardener found her slumped in a chair on the front verandah. He noted that an empty Scotch glass—

her regular afternoon practice—was on the table beside her.

Jacob and Charlotte reminisced about their childhood holidays as they sat with their parents in the foyer of the solicitor's office.

"Probably had one too many Scotches," Charlotte's father said.

"I'm pleased to hear the glass was empty," her mother bantered.

When the will was read, Charlotte tried hard to stop the tears flowing. Aunt Lucille had been like her second mother. They were kindred spirits; each understood the other. They'd spend hours walking around the Sydney house together. Talking about the collection of paintings that adorned the high walls. Together they had scrutinised the well-known artists, such as Sidney Nolan, Pro-Hart, and Aunt Lucille's favourite, the richly coloured paintings of Margaret Olley. The assortment of artwork hung side-by-side with Lucille's and Bernard's work and much to Charlotte's delight, Jacob and her own art pieces were also exhibited in between the others, as if they were just as important.

The solicitor read the will, the words blurred as Charlotte fought back her tears. Most of what he said didn't register, the details lengthy. It wasn't until they returned home to her parent's place that the enormity of what she had inherited, sunk in.

Charlotte and Jacob stared at each other, wide-eyed. They had been left the bulk of the will and contents of the house and cottage, with their parents receiving a large amount as well as several family items from the home. It was a substantial inheritance and more money than she could ever imagine belonging to one person. It would set her up for the rest of her life.

The Sydney house had been sold and everything finalised. All Charlotte needed to do was decide where she wanted to go. When the property near Bindarra Creek caught her eye, she followed up with an enquiry. The real estate agent, Hunter Sullivan, had been relaxed and helpful. The place needed a bit of work but not too much, it wasn't far from the small town and with the main house, a variety of sheds and four cabins that were zoned for commercial activities, the deal was sealed. It sold itself.

Perfect. A new career, a different area that wasn't too far from her family, and a new home far enough away from the Gold Coast so that she wouldn't run into Hugh and Bimbo.

———

CHARLOTTE THOUGHT about Aunt Lucille as she woke up on the first morning in her new home. Sunlight filtered in through the loungeroom window and she lay on her back, staring at the ceiling. An embossed diamond pattern circled a light, the bulb hanging down on a long black cord. The ceilings were solid plaster and picture rails ran around the walls, their narrow shelves decorating the chamferboard surfaces. Ornate timber arches painted in different colours led the way to other rooms and hallways.

She closed her eyes, excited to wake up in a place that belonged to her. Any decisions, both big and little were hers alone. No doubt there would also be mistakes, but at least they would be hers to make.

A sudden, loud pounding on the front door startled her and she sat upright. She'd thrown on the first dry piece of clothing she could find last night, an old T-shirt of Lucille's with splashes of paint across it, the length of it barely covering the top of her legs. Grabbing a pair of shorts from her bag, she jumped up, hurrying to get her legs into them as she called out to whoever was at the door.

"Just a minute."

Pushing her hair back from her face, Charlotte thought what a sight she must be. Her hair which was an out-of-control tangle of blonde curls at the best of times, was wild and woolly this morning, the hairband that usually kept it in some sort of order, lost amongst the blankets and sleeping bag.

She ran her hands over her T-shirt, tucked her hair behind her ears, and opened the front door.

"Good morning," called Hunter, thrusting a bottle of champagne and a bunch of flowers into her hands. "Welcome to Bindarra Creek."

"Thank you, and oh, they're lovely. I love native flowers." Charlotte smiled as she pushed her nose into the colourful blooms, clasping the bottle tightly, aware there was another man standing behind Hunter.

"And this is your neighbour, Alex. He let you in last night. I thought I'd bring him over to meet you properly."

Alex held out a hand, his tanned fingers closing over hers as she took it. Dark brown eyes stared into hers, a faint smile on his face. There was a rough stubble on his cheeks and she admired his short dark hair, seeming to sit exactly where it should. Neat and tidy, just like how he was dressed. She shook his hand before letting go and attempting to tuck her wild hair behind her ears.

"Pleased to meet you again," he said. "Apologies for last night. That gate has never been locked. That was bad timing with the storm."

She gestured for them to follow her into the house. "Oh, no worries. Nothing went right yesterday so that was just another stumble. No big deal."

No big deal, she thought, considering she could have been struck by lightning or died from a falling tree smashing into her car.

"Makes life exciting," she added. "Welcome to the palace. As you can see the furniture is still to be set up." The two men cast their eyes around the empty rooms.

"The cleaners did a good job," Hunter said. "At least that's something you don't have to worry about."

Charlotte placed the flowers and bottle on the kitchen bench. "They did. I'm in no hurry. I'll just unpack slowly and enjoy settling in."

Alex walked around the kitchen, running his hand over the walls. "Built to last these old houses. This one's a beauty."

"You're lucky, Charlotte." Hunter opened the back door. "Alex considered buying this place at one stage. His sister and her partner live in a cottage down the back of his property. They were keener than him, I'd say."

Turning to Alex she pulled her shoulders back and once again tried to push her hair behind her ears. "Well, I'm glad you didn't. This place suits me perfectly."

He shrugged. "I didn't need more land or buildings. I've enough to deal with what I've got."

"Lucky for you Charlotte, Alex's fiancée, Belinda, doesn't like old houses."

Alex shrugged. "Yes, that was interesting, Hunter, wasn't it? When you tried to point out all the positives to her. She struggles enough with my house, even though it's got more room than anyone could ever need. She's got plans drawn up for a new house, a more modern style."

"Oh, what will you do with the other one?" Charlotte said. "I saw it from the road the first time Hunter showed me this place. It's a beautiful old house."

"We haven't got that far yet. If I have my way it won't be going anywhere. That'd mean there would be two large houses on the property." He shook his head and she could see that he wasn't keen on the idea.

"Your mate, Lester, was the one who wanted this place," Hunter added. He turned to Charlotte. "You'll soon get to know everyone. Lester is married to Alex's sister, Bridie."

Alex interrupted, a scowl on his face. "They aren't married."

There was disdain in his voice and she wondered if it had been Lester in the car with him last night. Her eyes followed him as he walked towards the fireplace. The friendly tone returned to his voice. "I do love this old place. Are you going to change much?"

"Not anything too drastic. I'll maintain what's here and fix up a few things. I love this house and I want to try and keep the ambience of the place. That's what drew me here to begin with. I'm going to turn it into a writer's and artist's retreat. That will mean doing up the four cabins, so there will be plenty to keep me busy."

There was a pleasant tone to his voice and he

seemed pleased with her answer. His voice was deep and gentle, his manner welcoming.

He nodded. "Sounds like a plan. Just remember, Belinda and I are right next door if you need anything. Here's my card with my number on it, just in case."

She watched the two men as they got in the car and drove away. It sounded like she had been lucky to purchase the place. Thank goodness for Aunt Lucille's inheritance.

Chapter 3

The first items Charlotte brought in from the car were her electric jug and teapot. If she could have a cup of tea she'd be able to function and think about what needed to be done first. Hunter and Alex hadn't stayed long and although the welcome was friendly she was pleased to be left by herself to sort out the contents of her car. She liked her new neighbour, Alex. He seemed like a genuine guy, and not knowing anyone else from town, except for Hunter, it might be handy for her to have a local couple to turn to if there was anything she needed. The removal van was supposed to arrive in an hour or so and she needed to be dressed and ready to instruct them where to put everything. She glanced around the rooms again, grateful she didn't have to worry about cleaning. They were spotless.

Three stairs leading from the wide back verandah were a perfect place to sit and sip a hot cup of tea. A few leftover biscuits from the drive yesterday were still crunchy and she congratulated herself on finding something edible for breakfast.

The sky was clear, a bright blue stretching from one horizon to the other. Rays of winter sunshine warmed her legs and arms, the clear weather in direct contrast to what she had experienced last night. After the storm, the grass glistened and the trees and even the old sheds seemed to sparkle in the morning light. In front of her, a large house yard stretched out; a couple of sheds and a Hills hoist the only structures nearby. A variety of trees and gardens were scattered around the edges of the yard and she glanced up at the massive poinciana tree that stretched its limbs over one entire corner of the yard.

Her gaze fixed on the rickety treehouse perched on two of the wide horizontal limbs, wooden steps leading up to it nailed to the thick solid trunk. She'd spotted the treehouse when she'd first viewed the property, immediately loving the ancient tree that reminded her of one that she and Jacob had spent many hours climbing, the branches similar to a tree that rambled across the back boundary of Aunt Lucille's yard.

The view from this yard was different from that one, but similarly, a landscape you could stare at for hours. The house was situated on a small rise and beyond the house yard, the land sloped gently away towards the northern reaches of the property. Long grass filled the paddocks and Charlotte was impatient to walk around and explore.

Shading her eyes from the sun she spotted a small hummock towards the back end of the property. Four timber cabins stood in a row, their tin roofs glimmering in the sun. That was going to be one of her priorities, to start doing them up. After all, that was where her income was eventually going to come from. Beyond the cabins, tall trees bordered a winding creek; Hunter had told her there were deep pools there that were perfect for swimming. She tipped her cup up, relishing the last of the warm liquid.

Further over she could see the border of Alex's property. White fences ran around the perimeter and if she stood on the end of her verandah she could see his white, very large house, the house yard bordered by stiff, thin conifers that looked like they belonged more on the ritzy canal estates where she came from on the Gold Coast. From what Hunter told her, Alex's two-hundred-hectare estate had once been a rundown farm. He'd bought it six years ago and spent a large amount of money paying contractors to renovate it. The locals referred to it as, the Lord's House. Thea, at the Cyprus Cafe had told Charlotte the estate was regularly frequented by the rich, jet-setting polo groups who lived mainly in the big cities of Melbourne and Sydney. The owner, Alex, she explained, was one of those rich city folk who liked to dabble in country estates. She'd seen it all before. They usually bought the properties, renovated what was there, and then built a mansion where they could live for certain months of the year.

"They come, they go," she'd quipped as she passed Charlotte a sandwich. It was the same day that Charlotte had bought Forrest Glen and she tried to remember exactly what Thea had said. "Him and his famous fiancée, they just have these places as toys. It doesn't worry any of us here in Bindarra Creek though. At least when they have their fancy weekend events it brings money into the town." She'd leaned over the counter and lowered her voice. "Even though he's rich and won't stay, he is very good looking." She looked around the café to make sure no one had heard. "Sorry, don't mind me, but wait until you get a look at him."

Charlotte had not given the owners next door another thought after that. Her focus was on how she was going to transform her property into a sought-after retreat for writers and artists. Even though she had enough money from Aunt Lucille that she probably never needed to work again, she wanted to have something to aim for. With finances to back her, the new property would hopefully, eventually provide her with an income.

She thought about the man next door, Alex. He'd looked exactly as she expected. In fact, she knew before she even met him. Thea had reached under the counter and pulled out a magazine that showed a photo of him and his fiancée. "He's so handsome. Look at him. Looks like a movie star with that chiselled chin and muscly physique. Do you remember Paul Newman?" She looked over her glasses at Charlotte. "Actually, a stupid question because you probably weren't even born when he was on the screen. You're closer to my Thalia's age. Anyway, look him up, because your neighbour, that's if you buy the place, well he looks exactly like him. The only difference is that Paul Newman had blonde hair and this Alex fella has dark hair. The article gives all their details. You know, where they live, who they mix with."

Remembering the conversation, Charlotte googled the actor, Paul Newman, on her phone. She raised her eyebrows. Goodness me, Thea was right, Alex did look just like the actor had when he was young. She was living next door to celebrities, the rich and famous of the polo group as well as Alex's fiancée who was well known for her roles on the soapies on television.

Charlotte put her phone down. That was enough snooping. She couldn't be bothered looking at pictures of who his fiancée was. What you looked like or what you owned didn't mean anything. It was reassuring to meet Alex and know there were people next door she could turn to for help if needed, however she didn't intend to become too friendly with them. That sort of lifestyle was exactly what she wanted to get away from, and she'd already spent too much time thinking what a good looker he was

A truck's horn sounding out the front broke her daydream and she tipped the last of her tea out on the grass before making her way to the door

---

THE REMOVALISTS WORKED SOLIDLY, the two men patient as she directed them where to place the furniture and her most treasured pieces. Not everything had arrived in this first shipment, only those pieces. In the months before she moved, Jacob had enjoyed traipsing around the countryside with her, helping her locate what she needed. There was also furniture of Lucille's in storage and once she sorted out the first lot she'd work out what could go where. It was important that the furniture and household items coordinated with the era of the house and property. Everything was to be old or second-hand. No new fancy white or grey lounges, no glossy tiles, and definitely, no plastic outdoor furniture. Forrest Glen Retreat would be old world, with an atmosphere and living areas designed to match the pace the retreat would run at, slow and relaxed.

The previous owners had left kindling and firewood in one of the sheds and that night Charlotte lit the fire. Her old lounge chair, covered in the patchwork quilt Lucille had given her years ago was suited perfectly for snuggling up in front of the flames and she sank back into the chair, holding a glass of red wine in hand. Life couldn't get much better and even though the rooms were still full of unpacked boxes and bits of furniture were stacked untidily against the walls, she'd managed to create a couple of corners of comfort in amongst the mess. This room was warm and cosy, her blankets from last night bundled up next to her. She'd bunk down on the lounge tonight. Her bed was up, thanks to the removalists, but she hadn't time to make it, so sleeping in the warmth didn't seem like a bad option.

The fire crackled and glowed in the fireplace as the flames licked the dry logs she'd found in the shed and she soaked in the warmth as she munched on some left-over pizza that she'd brought with her. Tomorrow she'd do some more unpacking and go into town and stock the fridge and pantry. There was so much to do, both inside and out; she was never going to be bored living here. Charlotte closed her eyes, excitement filling her as she dreamed about the months, the years ahead.

A retreat.

If only Aunt Lucille was still alive. She would love this place. Charlottes' eyes grew heavy and she drank the last of the wine before crawling into her sleeping bag still wearing the same clothes she'd had on from the night before.

The best part was that she didn't have to worry

about anyone else. Who cared or would even know that she had worn the same clothes or hadn't brushed her hair for two days? If this was how it felt to be free, she was going to remain single forever.

Freedom, she thought as she shut her eyes, falling asleep before her head hit the pillow.

Chapter 4

The following days were filled with activity. Most rooms were now sorted and her bedroom was finally set up. With Jacob's help, she had picked out pieces of furniture from Lucille's before the rest was sold. Her favourite piece was the large four-poster bed, that stood in the middle of her bedroom. The four twisted cedar posts matching in style to a sideboard, hall stand and chaise lounge. Luckily, the rooms in the house were spacious and able to accommodate some of the larger pieces. A Persian rug was soft underfoot, the scent of Lucille's beloved Scottish Terrier, Buddha, faintly distinguishable in its coarsely woven surface.

Pushing a broom back and forth across the timber verandah Charlotte gazed across the paddocks. A small girl, aged about six was skipping, her knees kicked high as she went. Beside her, a taller boy, around eight, ran and jumped, racing around her. They stopped when they got to the fence, the boy helping the girl to climb over it.

As the children neared Charlotte's house she

wondered if they were Alex's children. Thea had been up with the town gossip and said he had a boy and girl, probably around the age these two were. They both went to boarding school and were only home on school holidays. There was no mother.

These must be the children she'd referred to. They waved at her and called out as they ran across the nearest paddocks, before long, both bounding up the steps in front of her.

The little girl was red in the face, her blonde hair tied up in two bouncy pigtails. She was cute as a button, with big dimples and a chubby smiling face. Her brother was also a good-looking boy, his blonde hair cut short, but the same dimples and green eyes as his sister, staring straight at her as she smiled and said hello. They stood before her, the girl with her hands on her hips and the boy stretching out his hand for her to shake.

"Hello," Charlotte said. "Who do we have here?"

"I'm pleased to meet you," the boy said. "My name is Eli and this is my younger sister, Isla."

"Pleased to meet you, Eli, and you also Isla." Charlotte held out her hand, shaking Eli's hand and then Isla's.

Both children wore expensive clothes; Isla's cotton floral dress matched with a bright red jacket over the top while Eli's shorts were ironed and a collared shirt tucked in neatly under a winter jacket. New shoes and long socks completed their outfits, their hair neat and their faces clean.

Isla looked Charlotte up and down. "We live next door. Our dad owns the polo horses and we have a dog called Jasper and two cats, Ethel and Milfred. We also have a swimming pool and I just got a pogo stick that I can jump on. My dad has lots of horses and people say he's the best person at breeding foals. What's your name?"

"My name is Charlotte. It must be wonderful having all those animals."

"It is but Belinda-Maree won't let them inside." Isla pouted when she spoke, her green eyes flitting back and forth as she tried to peer past Charlotte in through the doorway.

"Oh dear, that's not much fun, is it?"

"Do you have animals?" Eli took a step forward, also trying to get a better look inside."

Charlotte smiled at their inquisitiveness. "No. Not yet. I've just moved in so maybe one day I will."

Isla chatted incessantly. "Do you have a husband? We don't have a mum, she left Dad for another dad and she doesn't visit us. Now we're going to get a new mum, Belinda-Maree, but we don't like her and she's fussy and goes mad at us when we make a mess. When I spilled my drink last night, she…"

"Ssh," Eli butted in. "Remember Dad said you weren't to repeat everything. He told you what happens at home is private."

Charlotte grinned. "Would you like a cold drink?"

"Yes please," they both said at the same time.

They followed her into the kitchen, Isla talking nonstop.

"Dad let us come home from boarding school a bit earlier. He said we can have eight weeks here with him before going back. Belinda-Maree wasn't happy about that and I know because I followed them and hid behind the lounge while they were talking. She said we should go back early so she can have time with Dad by herself.

Dad said, we'll see. She doesn't like us, especially me. She says I talk too much. This is yummy. Lemonade is my favourite."

"Thank you," Eli said, putting his finger to his lip trying to get Isla to be quiet.

"Looks like someone is looking for you." Charlotte pointed across the paddocks. An older man followed the same path the children had. He stopped when he got to the fence, bending down to get through the wire and then straightening up slowly before walking toward them. He waved as he neared and Charlotte poured another cold drink from the jug as he made his way up the back stairs.

Isla jumped up and hugged his legs. "Barney, you came to visit Charlotte too."

Charlotte passed the old man a glass, his weathered hands reaching out to accept it.

"G'day. I'm Barney. I'm the caretaker next door. I came looking for these two. You turn your back for a minute and they're gone. He sipped the cool drink, sitting down on the bench seat beside Charlotte.

Barney's tattered hat sat crooked on his head, a sun-beaten face with deep-set eyes peering out from under it. His wiry arms were tanned dark from the sun, his short, muscled legs pushed into a well-worn pair of work boots.

She shook his hand. "I'm pleased to meet you, Barney."

"I meant to get over and introduce myself anyway. Now if you need anything, just sing out. I'm always around and can help. I live in a cottage down the back of Alex's property. I've been there forever. Worked there before he bought it." He ran his hand over the timber rail in front of him. "This is a beautiful property. I hear you're going to turn it into a retreat."

There was a gentleness about Barney and she loved the respectful way he bobbed his head towards her when he spoke, pouring her a drink from the jug, before taking another for himself.

"I love art, as does my brother Jacob," she said. "He'll come and stay sometimes once I've settled in. He's a writer, so a retreat for artists and writers was a perfect venture. There's plenty of work to do on the cabins but the place has so much potential."

Isla pulled at Barney's arm. "Can you come with me to the big tree over there? It looks like there is a cubby-house in it."

Barney pushed some hair back from her face and picked some cobbler peg prickles that were attached to her socks.

"Go and have a look for yourself. You're a big girl now. Take Eli with you and see if it's safe and not going to fall down. Go on, off you go."

Isla waited until Eli walked with her, the two of them making their way to the tree. Eli tested the bits of timber nailed onto the trunk, before climbing up them and telling Isla it was safe. The little girl followed, looking back at Barney and Charlotte with every step. Both children were hesitant and it took them a long while to pluck up the courage to go higher and find their way to the platform that made up the base of the tree-house. When they reached it they sat in the middle of it, peering cautiously over the edge.

Barney turned to her. "They don't get to do anything themselves. If it was up to me I'd have them in old clothes and bare feet. Fancy making kids wear shoes around the yard. I tried to tell Alex they won't have the confidence to do things but he follows everything that Belinda woman says. Anyway, you don't need to know all about that."

She laughed. "The kids have only been here half an hour but I think they may have filled me in on quite a few things."

Barney's eyes followed them as they crawled along the wide branch, Eli helping and cajoling Isla when she got stuck. "They're beaut kids. Spoilt rotten by Alex when they're here though. That Belinda gives them a bit of a hard time. She thinks I'm old and doddery and that I don't notice, but nothing much gets past me. You know their mother left when Isla was just two years old? She never came here much but said she'd had enough of life where they were also living in Sydney and up and left him. It's a rare thing for a mother to leave her kids behind. She met another man. A rich Italian man from the Amalfi Coast. Left Australia with him and never looked back. Every year she sends them a birthday card with a cheque in it. That's it though. Not another word." He turned to her. "You got kids, love?"

"No, Barney. I don't. I'm not married anymore. It's just me and not even any pets. I tell you what, I'm not hating it either. I was married but that didn't work out. I plan to make this place my life. I don't need anyone else."

He raised his eyebrows, looking like he was going to say something but then didn't. They sat and talked for a while and Charlotte was surprised to discover that Barney also loved to paint. "Used to dabble a bit. Many years ago. When my Mavis was still alive. I'll show you some of my paintings one day."

"That's fabulous, Barney. Do you still paint?"

He shook his head and looked down at the ground. When he looked up his eyes were full of sorrow. "I haven't picked up a paintbrush since the day she died. We were together sixty-two years. I miss her every day and I just don't have the heart to paint. It doesn't interest me anymore. Actually, lots of things don't."

Charlotte sat up straight as a car drove in beside the house.

Barney stood up, putting his hat back on his head. "Looks like these kids have got everyone out looking for them," he said. "That's Alex and his sister's partner, Lester. Now we'll be in trouble."

Isla and Eli stood up, yelling out to their father as he hopped out of the car. "Dad, Dad. Look at us. We're up in the treehouse."

Isla jumped up and down. "Look at me, Daddy. Look how high it is."

Alex rushed over and stood beneath them. "Okay, now stand still and don't be scared. I'll get you down. Sit back down and I'll lift you."

Barney winked at Charlotte, his voice low so Alex couldn't hear. "See what I mean. They can get down by themselves. They just need to climb down the same way they went up."

Alex lifted Isla down first and then Eli. Neither Barney nor Charlotte had moved and they watched as he held their hands and led them up towards the verandah. The other man who had been in the car also made his way toward them.

Alex sounded a bit stern when he spoke and Charlotte tried not to giggle as he admonished both the children. What a worrier, she thought. If only he could see what kids did once they were let loose at school. She listened to him as he continued to give instructions. "You must not get up into high places like that or leave the house without telling me where you're going. Please always remember the rule that you aren't to go beyond our property fence or through any of the gates. The land beyond that is not ours. I want you to apologise for coming here uninvited."

Barney stood up, taking his hat off and banging it against his leg. He replaced it before stacking the glasses together near the jug. "I wasn't far behind them. They just went exploring."

Alex smiled at her. "Hello, Charlotte. Thank you for watching over them."

She waited for him to introduce the other man but he must have forgotten she hadn't already met him. She peered at him from behind her sunglasses. There was something vaguely familiar about him but she wasn't sure what it was.

He nodded at her, his unsmiling face sending a chill down her spine. Where did she know him from and why did she have an instant distrust, or was it instinctive dislike?

Barney caught her eye and she realised she was staring. "This is Lester," Barney said. "I don't think you've met him yet."

She nodded back at Lester. "Pleased to meet you."

He squinted at her and nodded, before turning his face away to talk to Alex. "C'mon, I've got work to do. I can't waste any more time running after these bloody kids."

Isla and Eli stood silently, clutching their father's hand. Charlotte picked up instantly that the children were not fond of Lester and her mind ticked over as she watched them all get into the car.

"I'd love it if you let them come this far to see me. I used to be a primary school teacher and I miss the company of kids this age."

Isla jumped up and down, tugging on her father's hand and Eli also looked up at him. "I'll look after Isla, Dad. It's not very far from our place."

"As long as it's okay with Charlotte, I don't mind. But you need to remember you aren't to go any further than here."

Isla grinned at Charlotte who pursed her lips in amusement. It was obvious that Alex doted on the children and perhaps like most little girls, Isla was able to twist him around her little finger.

"Come and play anytime," she said, waving to them through the back windows of the car where they sat with Alex.

Alex chuckled, seeming relaxed now he had his kids safely with him and he was once again in control. "Don't tell them that they'll be here all the time."

"I don't mind at all," she replied, laughing as Isla blew her kisses.

She glanced quickly at Lester, his face set and his eyes turned away from her. He seemed nervous, fidgety, as he twisted a charm attached to his leather bracelet. Interesting, she thought as she watched as the car drove back out the driveway and through the gate, turning up the easement towards the house next door.

There were a variety of people who lived on Alex's property. The children were adorable and Barney was such a gentleman; the type of person you could sit and talk to all day. As for Lester, she didn't like the look of him one bit. The image of his face stuck in her mind, a persistent nagging pressing on her. She'd seen him somewhere before. Perhaps he'd lived on the coast at some stage. Barney would know. Next time she saw him, she'd ask. Now she needed to get back into sorting out the boxcs and setting up. The days would fly and Jacob would be here to help her before she knew it. Together they'd get the place organised and then would come the exciting part.

The retreat.

Chapter 5

Alex sat in the back of the car on the way home. Isla had crawled onto his lap. Wrapping his arms around her he kissed the top of her head, enjoying that she was still little enough to cuddle and carry. Both kids were growing up too fast. If only he could keep them at this age for longer. Now that they were at school he saw them less and less.

Isla looked up at him with her big innocent eyes and he spoke softly in her ear. "Don't ever get too big that you don't want to give me cuddles."

He was rewarded with a kiss.

"Never," she said, giggling quietly before cupping her hands around his ears and whispering. "Look, Lester's neck is like a bush turkey's."

Alex clenched his teeth to stop his laughter. Isla was right. Red rolls of skin crossed the back of Lester's neck and spiky bits of hair stuck out from them. It was strange that there was fat there because Lester was skinny. There was also a tattoo amongst the folds of skin but it was faded and hard to tell what it was.

Squeezing Isla tighter he shook his head at her. He'd had various conversations with her about commenting on Lester's looks or ways. Only yesterday she'd started talking about him, and Alex had struggled to get her to stop once she started.

"Lester always spies on us," she'd said, the cute pout on her face stopping Alex from what he'd been doing. "Not just me, but Eli and you. He slinks around like the sloth in my picture books. He has beady eyes and thin lips and looks like an evil cartoon character. I hate him, more than I hate my teacher."

"That's enough, Isla. Remember what I said, if it's not nice don't say it."

She'd stomped her foot. "When Lester is near me I get prickles on my skin. He's not nice."

Alex had wanted to agree with her, there was certainly something about Lester that also put him on edge. "I've heard you, Isla, but that's enough now. Just keep clear of him."

Now as they drove back towards home he thought about how he was always trying to keep everyone happy. His sister often complained that the kids didn't come and see her but Alex had told them on numerous occasions not to visit Bridic at her house or be down in the stables unless he was with them.

They were only here for the holidays and once they were back at boarding school he didn't need to worry about them being around Lester or going on the property where they shouldn't. There was two hundred hectares for them to roam but he wanted them near the house and with him when they were here. That wasn't always easy, because Belinda-Maree also wanted him to herself. It was obvious that Isla and Eli weren't overly keen on his fiancée. The fact that she hadn't had much to do with kids previously had made the interactions difficult and he'd tried hard to get everyone to like each other. No doubt that part was going to take a while, especially for Isla who had also unfortunately overheard Belinda-Maree telling him that she thought the kids were too clingy and needed to be doing more without him.

He sighed, watching Isla as she glared at the revision mirror. Lester was looking at it also, his eyes narrowing as he stared back. Lester looked back down when Alex caught his gaze. Isla's face was set in a scowl and she snuggled back into his chest as the car pulled up in front of the house.

There was more to Lester than met the eye and if it wasn't for the fact that Bridie seemed happy with him, Alex would have long ago told him to move on. Even Eli had picked up on his nasty side and had told Alex how he and Isla sometimes followed Lester across the paddocks.

"It was Isla's idea, Dad," Eli said. "She thinks she's one of those detectives like she reads about in the books at school. If she lays down and crawls through the grass she says he can't see us. We had to hide behind some trees, to make sure. The trouble was once he went through the back of Charlotte's place, there weren't any trees to hide behind. We crouched behind the old shed and watched him go through the furthest gate. He kept walking towards the mountains. Isla thinks he's doing something sneaky."

"Don't ever follow him again and make sure Isla doesn't either. I'll have a talk to her."

Alex thought about that conversation now as he

watched Lester get out of the car. Why would he go out through the property next door? It wasn't as if he liked walking and the mountains were a far distance away. Strange, Alex thought. He'd have to keep an eye on that, and Isla.

As they got out of the car, Isla gripped Alex's hand as Lester patted the bonnet of the car. "Five times," Isla said quietly so that no one but Alex could hear. "Always five times."

As he stood and watched Lester walk away towards the cottage he lived in with Bridie, he reminded himself to watch him more closely. Eli and Isla meant everything to him and he didn't care if Belinda-Maree thought he was over cautious. Lester put him on edge.

Isla tugged on his hand as Belinda-Maree came out of the house to greet them. "Can we look at the horses, Dad?"

"Your father needs to come and sit down and have a chat with me," Belinda-Maree answered before he could. "Run along, there's a good girl. Give him some space."

He took a deep breath. Theirs had been a whirlwind romance. Belinda-Maree had swept him off his feet with her exquisite looks and interesting personality. He'd only had a handful of girlfriends since the children's mother had left and he'd made sure not to get too involved with any of them. His life had been shattered when he'd been left with two small children to look after and a marriage breakup that he hadn't seen coming. The last thing he'd wanted was another relationship.

Belinda-Maree was different though. She'd made him laugh and helped him regain some of his love of life. For years he'd focused on his work in Sydney, the polo business and property, breeding, competing and socialising when he had to. She'd stormed into his life and taken over. He hadn't minded and when she started to make more and more decisions he let her have her way. It had been a long time since anyone had done that and he'd gone along with her ideas for the children to attend boarding school, the changes she wanted in the house and when she'd suggested that they get engaged and married in the coming year, he'd agreed. She was fun to be with and he still got plenty of time to himself while she concentrated on her acting career.

Now it was school holidays and the kids were home, life had not been so smooth. He'd argued with her and stood his ground when she tried to stop the kids staying for the extra weeks. "I want them here for two months," he'd said, ignoring her sulky look and harsh words.

"Sometimes, Alex, I wonder who the most important person is in your life? Is it me or them?"

"My children are, and they always will be."

They'd argued that night and he'd tried to explain that she needed to think of them as her family too.

"I don't understand why you don't let Bridie do more for them. She has access to all your money to get everything for them."

The argument had grown heated and in the end he'd walked away, leaving her drinking her wine alone.

Now he followed her up to the courtyard where he could see she had drinks and nibblies set out for them. Isla and Eli had taken off upstairs and he took one last look at Lester, before giving Barney a wave goodbye.

It was never easy keeping everyone happy.

Chapter 6

Lester sat alone in the small office at the rear of the stables. He'd moved away from the others and the car as quickly as he could, ensuring that he patted the bonnet five times before distancing himself from those pesky brats. That Isla kid talked way too much and she was always watching him.

There weren't many jobs that he did around Alex's property but right from when he arrived he'd volunteered to clean the office. That way he could shut the door, make a cup of tea and have the space to himself. The room was rarely used and it gave him a chance to be by himself and use the phone if he needed to.

He lit a cigarette, drawing back deeply, relieved to be in a silent room. That's what he liked the most. Being by himself. Soon his life would get back to that, just him, and he wouldn't have to put up with those kids spying on him, or anyone else near him. That was one thing he was sure of, and also, that before the month was out he'd be as far away from Bindarra Creek as possible.

Soon he'd be set up for life. Western Australia was

looking good. If only he could keep that kid from watching him all day.

He smiled and stirred his cup of tea, three times to the left and then three times to the right. The spoon clinked two times on the cup and then two times on the saucer before he laid it down gently on the left-hand side of the table. He sipped it slowly. Strong, black, and full to the brim. Always the same. It had to be. Otherwise, he'd have bad luck.

That had been his downfall when the cops caught up with him last time. He'd become lazy, less vigilant, and not focused on his routines. As he took another sip of his tea he thought about how he'd cursed himself by killing that bloody chook. It was a stupid move because there had been blood. Everything was supposed to die a natural death. And he knew, blood, and killing, brought nothing but a curse. Even though he buried the hen, placed a cross on the spot and recited a poem for it, the jinx was set. The cops arrived the next day and arrested him. They said they'd had a tip-off.

He should have been more careful. All the years he'd managed to avoid them, but now because of his stupid temper he'd broken his rules that were strict on the protocols of superstitions and curses. He fondled the cross that hung from his ear. They hadn't let him wear it in jail. That or his plaited leather wristband with a lucky four-leaf clover hanging from it. The possessions had been there in the paper bag they gave him the day he walked out a free man. He'd waited until he was clear of the prison boundaries before putting them both on.

He twirled the earring the right number of times and said a few words to his clover and faced it to the front. It wouldn't happen again. This time he'd be on his toes and ensure nothing led to him doing more time. He shuddered at the thought. He wasn't going back into that hole again. Dumb coppers, he thought. They'd only got him on some crimes. If only they knew about the bigger ones. They'd been watching him, waiting for him to make the wrong move. But he was way smarter than they were.

He smiled as he turned his cup in his hand, twice to the left and twice to the right. Placing it down gently on the saucer with the handle facing the back, he thought about how clever he'd been to change his appearance, buy new identification documents and make his way back to Bindarra Creek. Nothing much had changed over the years. He'd lived down this way when he was in his early twenties.

Back then was when he'd originally discovered the hideout. Someone in town mentioned that the elderly couple who owned the property, called Forrest Glen, were looking for a handyman to do some light work. They'd lived on the run-down farm forever and knew the mountains on their boundary like the back of their hand.

It wasn't often that he did honest work but the word was that the couple had a broad knowledge of the area and talked about bushranger hideouts in the mountains that bordered the far reaches of their property. He'd thought it sounded interesting, worth checking out. And it had been. Although they no longer ventured past the yard, they told him about places they'd discovered in earlier years, when they were younger. The area was smattered with secret hideouts, where bushrangers had once hidden from the law, many years before, in a different century. The couple, excited that someone was interested in the folklore of the area, drew him a map and assured him that no one else knew how to get in or out of there. Years ago, there had been another track in, but that had long gone. They were too old now to walk that far and the only easy way to access the area was through their property.

Lester could lay on the charm when needed and pretended that he was interested in the local history, the legends of the bushrangers, and the heritage of the area. The information he gained was detailed and after he'd finished the maintenance work for them he'd followed their directions and found exactly what he was looking for.

———

DENSE SCRUB BLOCKED the way to the creek at the far end of the property and beyond that, the hills rose sharply, their steep sides and thick bush a deterrent to anyone who might ever venture in that direction. He knew no one would ever find their way in and out of where he went. A shiver of excitement pulsated through his body. He, Lester McLean was the only one who knew the spot.

Now it was August and time to leave. Bridie had served his purpose well. Her and her stupid rich brother. He hadn't even bothered to steal from her, she gave him whatever he wanted; a steady supply of cash that her brother allowed her access to and an endless bank account to buy whatever was needed for his brats. Just bide your time, he reminded himself, don't draw attention to your activities. He'd make sure he had a clean run. He'd leave Bridie a note, saying they were done. He could just walk away, take what was his and begin his life on the other side. He'd change his name again.

He stubbed out his cigarette in a small tin he always carried with him. Nothing went on the ground. It wasn't that he cared about rubbish, the point was it was bad luck to put tobacco or the ash back into the earth. It meant that was your last cigarette. It would mean your time was up. Tipping the last of his tea down his throat he thought about how lucky he was that he knew how to keep the curses away. It had kept him alive, allowed him the convenience of living with Bridie, and to safely spend the waiting time in a comfortable manner at her brother's fancy farm.

He pushed his hat back on his head and twisted his wristband so that the clover sat to the front; always to the front. He was a fortunate man and soon he'd be even luckier and out on his own again with enough money to last him a lifetime. Gazing over the paddocks that separated the two properties he smirked, thinking about the new owner of Forrest Glen. What were the chances of him running into someone from his past? Clenching his fists and shaking his head to rekindle memories, he thought hard, trying to recall a particular day.

At least she didn't look like the sort who would venture into the wilderness behind the property. Her and those brats wouldn't be smart enough. No one would stand in his way, he'd make sure of that.

Chapter 7

Eli and Isla soon had a well-worn path through the paddocks to Charlotte's place. Following them was usually an array of animals; Jasper the dog, the two cats and sometimes a few ducks or geese. The scene reminded Charlotte of the Pied Piper and she described the fairy tale to Isla and Eli.

"You've heard those stories before, haven't you?" she asked, digging through one of the boxes to find her books. She turned the pages of a thick fairy tale book, grateful her mother had kept her childhood treasures. Isla choose one and Charlotte read the story out loud, surprised that they weren't familiar with it. "Can we take it up to the cubbyhouse?" the little girl asked.

"Of course, you can. As long as you look after them." Charlotte passed her three of her favourite hard-covered books.

Isla climbed up the wooden slats into the treehouse before lying on her stomach on the old boards and peering at the pages. No doubt she would love the coloured glossy pictures that accompanied the stories.

The dog and one of the cats lay underneath the tree, curled up together. The other cat had followed Isla and sat beside her, also looking at the pages as it licked its paws. Eventually, the cat lay down next to her, the backyard a quiet and serene sight. Eli was also kept busy when Charlotte discovered he loved nothing more than to make things out of timber. An old hammer and handsaw of her father's, along with pieces of cut-off pine resulted in a decent-looking box that he proudly presented her with before he and Isla headed off home. She displayed it on her table on the back verandah. "I'll keep my treasures in there," she told him, placing the timber lid that he had made, squarely on the box. "You're clever. This lid fits perfectly."

Alex rang after the first week. "The kids just want to come to your place all the time. I have a huge cubby-house here that cost a fortune. It's painted blue and has a kitchen, lounge and all the bits and pieces that go with it. Plus, it's on the ground. But no, they whinge and carry on when I say to play in there and then they disappear to your place. They must be eating you out of house and home."

"It's funny that you say that, because I was in town earlier and Mr Porter at the hardware shop asked me how I'd settled in and if I'd met you. I told him your kids had fallen in love with my poinciana tree and all they wanted to do was to play in the treehouse."

"I bet he had a laugh about that. He would have made a large profit out of the cubbyhouse I bought from him. I tell you, everyone knows everything about you around here. You can't get away with much."

"Yes, I got asked a run of questions when I went to

the IGA. I only wanted a few items but I was in there for ages."

"Someone new in town, the locals love it. Are you sure you have time for the kids to visit?"

Charlotte laughed. "It's okay, honestly. I'm out in the yard doing things anyway so they're never far away from me. Don't forget I was a teacher. I love kids, plus they're well-behaved. Maybe just make sure Isla wears a hat though."

"Thanks, Charlotte. I'll send Barney over when they need to come home. I worry about them walking through the paddocks if it starts to get dark. I've told them they have to be back before then."

"I make them leave before the sun goes down. Lester often watches out for them. I see him standing in the back paddock. He watches them walk home."

Alex didn't reply and she wondered if he had heard her. "Are you still there?"

"I am. Yes, still here. I'll make sure I get Barney to come over and walk them back each time. Can we please make that a rule that they aren't to leave your place until Barney comes to collect them? And it must be Barney, no one else."

She took a deep breath. Why was he so adamant it needed to be Barney and why had he only come up with that idea after she mentioned Lester? Perhaps it was best not to ask questions. Obviously, there were family problems or some issues with his sister and Lester. It was easy to pick up on those vibes from both the children and Alex.

"Okay, you tell them both and I'll make sure it happens."

They chatted for a bit longer and he asked how she was finding the new location compared to where she'd come from. She looked through the open door that led out onto the side verandah. In the distance, the mountains shimmered in the heat of the day, the edges of them hazy. Puffy heavy clouds hung low, their shadows darkening parts of the paddocks that stretched down to the creek beyond the gate. "It's a beautiful part of the world," she said, feeling euphoric. "I love the view to the west. Those mountains are amazing in the afternoon light. They turn all different colours as the sun goes down. Often your horses are in front of the setting sun. It's an artist's dream."

"Oh, that's right. You're an artist. Isla told me. Those mountains that your property runs to, border Akuna National Park. There's a variety of stories about the events that occurred in and around them many years ago. It's said they were the hangout of bushrangers and also where some of them were holed up before shootouts with the police. It's hard to know what's real and what's a myth."

"I'll have to go for a drive and check them out. Perhaps when my brother arrives."

"I'd love to take you both out there if you have time one day. I haven't been that way for years. You can walk there from here, but It's a fair distance. We used to visit my grandmother way over the other side of the park. There were similar areas there and as kids we played in and around the boulders and caves. Bushrangers and cops." He laughed, a sound she hadn't heard from him before. "I'd forgotten about those good times. Seems so long ago." His voice faded and she guessed that like her, there were memories that had been pushed aside after dealing with the tumultuous times that may have come afterward.

"Thanks again for letting the kids come and play. Belinda-Maree seems to think they should be in their yard, but they're not far away and for some reason, your place is way more attractive to them than their own."

She wanted to tell him why that was probably so, but it wasn't her problem that what they were allowed to do at his place was vastly different from what they could do at her place. She had rules and expectations when they were at her place although she'd never needed to discipline them or speak to them sternly. They were great kids and just wanted to play. They were also voracious readers and she'd messaged Jacob to make sure he brought the rest of her books with him when he came for his visit.

"I'm surprised no one reads to you," she said to Eli one day. The three of them sat up in the tree leaning back on the thick branches surrounding the treehouse. They sat on the floorboards and Charlotte brought up lemonade and freshly made pikelets with jam and cream.

Isla had a pikelet in each hand, cream and jam smeared across her face. She took another bite and Charlotte could tell she wanted to speak but knew she needed to wait until she finished eating what was in her mouth. She chewed faster, her eyes wide at the frustration of not being able to talk. Finally, she finished the mouthful.

"Barney will be here soon to get us. Maybe he could sit up here with us. He got angry with Belinda yesterday for nagging us about staying clean."

"It's Belinda-Maree," Eli added, rolling his eyes.

"You know she'll chuck a tantrum if you don't say her name right."

"I know her name. I'll say it how *I* want."

"You need to do what Dad says." Eli had put on his grown-up voice. "And not spy on Lester either."

"I hate Lester. He's always looking at me funny. I wish he'd run away."

Eli turned to Charlotte. "He is creepy. I don't like him either. Do you know he has all sorts of superstitions? Sometimes I hear him talking to himself, like he's crazy. Jasper growls when he comes near us."

"Everyone's different I guess," Charlotte replied, her nerves on edge from what they were saying. She didn't let on she had a bad feeling when she met Lester.

"Bridie should kick him out," Isla added. "He's not a nice man. Not like Barney. Barney's my friend and I think he should come and sit here and eat pikelets with us. You know I like Barney the most. I wish that he wasn't lonely and had a wife." She looked at Charlotte and squinted, her hair tied up in a high pigtail bobbing around on top of her head.

Most days both the children now wore old shorts and T-shirts, and although they came with shoes on they were quickly discarded and didn't go back on again until they went home. By the time they went home, they were also filthy and covered in dirt or paint. Isla patted her on the shoulder, making sure she had her full attention. "Is Barney too old for you to marry? You said you don't have a husband, maybe you could marry Barney."

Charlotte sat up straight and blinked hard. "Barney is a lot older than me, Isla. I think a lot of him, and he is my very good friend. He is much, much, older than me, and please don't say anything like that again. Also,

Barney still loves his wife. He's happy the way he is. I don't think he wants another wife."

"But she's dead and you're here and you don't have a husband. How can you love someone when they're dead?"

They all shuffled around on the boards, lying next to each other, flat on their backs, staring up through the canopy of the tree. Isla reached out and held Charlotte's hand, her small fingers soft on Charlotte's skin. "I still think you should marry Barney."

Charlotte thought hard. "When people get married they need to love each other and want to be with each other for the rest of their life. Barney wouldn't want to upset Mavis, because even though she's up in heaven she would still be looking down at him."

Isla sat up, her voice animated. "So, one day when he dies, he will meet up with her again, and then they can still be married." She hardly came up for breath. "Now, we need to find you another husband. That way you can get a dog and have a baby."

Charlotte laughed as she spoke. "Yes to Barney meeting up again with Mavis and, no, to another husband for me. I am very, very, happy with how I am, thank you. Not everyone needs to get married or have a partner for that matter. It's easy to be happy just living by yourself," Hopefully that would end the conversation about her marrying Barney or anyone else. She quickly changed the topic. "Look up at the tree, it's starting to ready itself for the spring months."

The tree was starting to lose its leaves, the tiny petal-like leaves falling like raindrops to the ground every so often. The boards beneath their bodies as well as the ground underneath the tree were covered in layers of faded orange petals and delicate leaves. Above them the clear August sky poked through the gaps in the branches, a circling hawk appearing now and again in its search for the field mice that scurried between the clumps of grass.

Isla was still not content with the way the conversation had ended. "You must need a husband and Barney needs a wife. Belinda-Maree told me that the most important thing is finding a husband."

Charlotte put on her teacher's voice. "That is not the most important thing in life. Some people, like me, are very happy making decisions for themselves and being independent. It's just like Barney, he wouldn't want another wife."

"You still love Chookers and he's dead," Eli said to Isla.

Chookers, their favourite bantam hen, had been eaten by a fox the week before.

Isla thought hard and seemed to take in what her brother said. "I do still love Chookers and I will always love Chookers forever and ever."

Charlotte interrupted her. Sometimes you had to, to get a word in edgeways. "Getting back to what I was talking about. I'm surprised no one reads to you at home or school."

Eli put on an American accent, stretching out his legs and shaking his body when he spoke. "Ain't nobody got time for that."

Charlotte giggled along with them, feeling like she was a kid again herself. "I read them myself because ain't nobody got time for that," Isla mimicked, placing the book down over her face. "Chookers is dead, Barney needs a wife and Charlotte needs a husband, and ain't nobody got time for that."

They all laughed and she looked downwards at their toes, all of them with no shoes on, her long legs stretched out and poking over the edge of the boards. Isla had brought a pot of dark fingernail polish with her today. Belinda-Maree had given it to her and told her not to show her father. Charlotte let Isla paint all their toenails and fingernails before hiding the bottle in the tree. Isla also arranged Charlotte's hair in pig-tails the same as hers and commented how Charlotte wore the same clothes as she did, tiny cotton shorts and a singlet top.

Charlotte laughed again and turned to Eli. "I'm supposed to be a grown-up, not a kid." She wriggled her toes and they both copied her. "I need to do housework and clean the floors but it's such a beautiful warm day."

"Ain't nobody got time for that," Eli said in the deepest voice he could muster.

Isla used a squeaky high voice. "Belinda said I must clean my room and pick my clothes up because she's not my slave."

"Ain't nobody got time for that," Charlotte and Eli said together.

Isla rolled over on her stomach and stroked Charlotte's face gently with the fronds from the leaves of the tree. It tickled and Charlotte squirmed and laughed when Isla repeated, "Chookers is dead, Barney loves his old wife and Charlotte doesn't need a husband, and ain't nobody got time for that."

The three of them laughed so hard that the boards of the cubbyhouse shook. Charlotte couldn't stop and tears rolled down her face as the children continued with their jokes. Their voices got louder and louder, their laughter contagious, as they tried to outdo each other with their words. Suddenly a loud "oi" startled them all and they sat up and peered over the edge of the boards. Alex stood below them, hands on hips and a comical scowl on his face.

Charlotte's face burned. How long had he been standing there, listening to her and his children make fun of all the rules and regulations of his household?

"Daddy," Isla squealed as she jumped up and rushed to the side. She threw her legs over and flung herself outwards, his arms quickly raised, catching her as she jumped. He swung her around, her little arms wrapped around his neck, hanging on as he squeezed her tight.

"Next time, warn me that you're going to jump." Alex looked up at Charlotte and she grinned back as a wide smile spread across his face. Eli grabbed a rope they had tied from a higher branch and swung his way down to the ground, a loud yeeha as he went, adding excitement to the arrival of their father.

Charlotte sat with her legs dangling over the edge, her bare feet covered in dirt much the same as the children's. She was lost for words, contemplating how loudly she'd giggled and carried on like a child. How was she supposed to know he was standing underneath and where was Barney?

"Where's Barney," was all she could think of to say.

"He's washing down one of the horses, so I said I'd come and get the kids."

"Oh."

He stood staring at her, Isla bouncing around in his arms.

"Is everything okay?" she asked.

He shook his head and hoisted Isla onto his shoulders, ignoring her squeals of delight. "Yes, um yes. Everything is fine. I just hadn't heard the kids laugh like that for a long time. For a very long time." He looked down at his feet and then back up to her again. "You have a natural way with these two. You sounded like a kid yourself. It must be good to let go like that and forget about everything else in life."

She swung herself down on the rope, grateful that she hadn't lost her footing or arm strength, and managed to land elegantly, and not flat on her face. She made it look like she came down that way all the time when actually she'd never been game too, in case the rope broke. Eli passed her the book she had been reading to them. "Thank you, Eli," she said brushing herself off.

Alex's face held an amused expression as he reached out and picked a twig from her hair. His gaze lingered on her and she found herself staring back into his smouldering eyes. He was a very handsome man, his face covered in a fine stubble, his tanned arms wrapped around Isla who was unusually quiet.

"Thank you," she said, trying to ignore the thumping of her heart and hoping like anything that he couldn't read her thoughts as he pulled another small stick from her hair. His voice was deep and she clenched her teeth and held her breath, her chest rising up and down as he continued to stare at her. A rush of heat flooded her body as she steadied her voice.

"It is good to forget about other matters. That's the best part about being with kids. They make you disregard everything else and if you enter their world you can regain a little of what it's like to be a child again.

Sometimes people grow older and cranky even at a young age." She thought about what she had just said. "Actually, I need to remind myself of that more often."

Alex looked at both the kids. "It's easy to slip into the adult serious role. I…" He stopped talking, shuffling his feet.

The silence was broken by Jasper who had been sleeping in the shade. He stretched one back leg and then the other, a sharp yap to let them know he was awake.

"Jasper's sleepy a lot, Daddy," Isla said as Alex put her down on the ground.

"He's getting old," Alex replied. "He didn't even stir when I arrived here. Not a great watchdog anymore."

Eli patted him and scratched under his chin. "You're not allowed to put him to sleep though. I heard you and Belinda talking. She said it's time for him to go to the vet."

Isla's eyes widened and a scowl covered her face. She wrapped her arm around Jasper who rewarded her with a lick on her cheek. She giggled, "You ain't going nowhere, Jasper. Ain't nobody got time for that."

Alex smiled. "C'mon you two. It's time to go home and leave Charlotte alone. You don't want her getting tired of you visiting." He looked down the side of the house. "Look, here's Barney come to collect us. That will save us walking. He can drive us all back."

Barney appeared, a wide grin across his face, as usual, his gait crooked as he made his way towards them. "You're in trouble at home all of you. Belinda-Maree said to come and collect you. You were all supposed to be back there by five."

"He's got two false hips," Eli said. "His body is full

of nuts and bolts under his skin. He says he'll fall apart if they rust, that's why he won't go swimming."

"Nothing wrong with my ears, Mr Eli. Don't go telling stories about me."

Charlotte remembered something she had promised to show Barney. "Have you got some time tomorrow, Barney? I'd love to show you some more of the paintings that were delivered yesterday. I haven't put them up yet, they're just stacked in the lounge. You're all welcome to have a look. Most of them belonged to my Aunt Lucille. She was an amazing artist."

She was surprised when Alex spoke up. "We'd all love to see the paintings. Why don't we have a look now? There's no hurry." He took Isla's hand and they all followed Charlotte up the stairs and into the lounge room.

Alex's eyes roamed around the room. "Wow, this has changed since the first day you moved in. It looks amazing. So much warmth and colour. I love those paintings that are already up."

"Thank you. It's a work in progress and I'll be pleased when I get these other ones hung. They're my most treasured possessions."

Both the children found their way to the bookcase, Isla pulling her favourite book out to look through. Alex frowned. It was obvious that both felt at home in Charlotte's house. She noticed him watching them. "We don't come inside much when the kids are here, we're mostly outside. They do love my books though."

"Look Dad," Eli said, "I'm going to read this one next. I have Book One at home. Charlotte let me borrow it."

Alex was surprised. "I didn't know you liked to read,

Eli. Remind me, somewhere up in the storage there's a heap of books I had when I was a kid. They haven't been out of those boxes for probably over twenty years."

Eli screwed his face up. "You have books from when you were a kid? How come you never showed me?" They stood staring at each other. It looked like Eli was about to storm out of the room. His face turned red and he clenched his fists.

"It's no big deal. I'll get them down for you," Alex replied.

Charlotte looked from one to the other. An argument was brewing. She turned to Eli. "Could you please help me with these? I need your muscles Eli so that I can show Barney the artwork." Eli took a deep breath, Charlotte grateful that Isla hadn't come out with her, "Ain't nobody got time for that".

Chapter 8

Eli separated the framed paintings and propped them against the wall. There were eight in the collection, four of which were quite large. He moved them back and forth, positioning them underneath where they might hang. It was obvious he was happy to be given some responsibility and allowed to make decisions about where to place them.

Alex walked slowly in front of them, looking closely at each one. Barney also took his time and no one spoke, apart from Isla who rarely was silent. After a while, Barney asked her to be quiet. "Just for a minute, love. These are amazing and I think we all want to look at them and think our own thoughts. We'll share what we like about them once we've finished looking."

She had huffed and puffed a bit and after having a good look at the artwork went back to the books.

Eli finally broke the silence. "Which one do you like, Dad?"

Alex ran his hand over his chin, thinking before deciding. "I can't quite decide. This is a Margaret Olley,

Eli. She was a very well-known artist and this picture is typical of her bright style." He stood back admiring the bold colours of the vase spilling over with vibrant coloured flowers before moving closer to another larger painting. "I do love this one though. The shades and lines on this watercolour are so entwined and it's a peaceful scene. Actually, the countryside reminds me of around here." He moved to the next one. "But then this small oil also draws me in. The lady in it is intriguing. Look at how exciting the clothing and furniture is and her face, well…" he turned his head from side to side, "almost as if she is looking right back at you and knows what you're thinking." He peered closer, before turning to Charlotte. "This is the artist, isn't it? It has to be."

She smiled. Up until now she had stayed quiet, silently giving herself a lecture about the flutters in her stomach each time Alex looked at her. He was engaged. She'd sworn off men; these feelings needed to disappear. Picking up the painting, she gathered her thoughts.

"You picked it. This is my beautiful Aunt Lucille. It's a self-portrait done not long before she passed away." She passed it to Alex, trying to ignore the tingling when his hand brushed against hers. His eyes widened and he held her stare.

"Um, yes, um, I thought it was."

It was obvious he was flustered and she wondered if he too had felt the heat as their skin touched.

Ridiculous, she thought, *get a grip*.

Alex finally pulled his gaze away from the painting, turning to Eli. "Now you tell me which one you like the most."

Eli walked up and down the line of paintings. A large unframed painting, completed on a piece of board stood separately from the rest. "I put this one away from the others because it doesn't match them."

Alex squatted down to see it more clearly. It was abstract, but behind the cubes and square lines was a girl's face. "It is very well done. An amazing piece but I think you're right. It is different than the others. So, son, do you like it or not?"

It was the first time that Charlotte had seen Alex talk to Eli like a grown-up and not a small child. She had only ever seen him discipline or lecture the children and her heart warmed to see the look on Eli's face. Eli stood up and stuck out his chin, running his hand over it, the same as his father had. Alex bit his lip as if to hold back a smile.

Eli stood back from it, turning his head from side to side. "I think it is very good but it makes me feel sad, not happy like the other ones make me feel. It's an angry painting."

"But the girl is smiling," Barney added. "She's lovely. I thought she looked happy."

Alex waded into the appraisal. "She looks happy but the painting is angry. Whoever painted it was irritated."

Charlotte pulled a couple of sheets of paper from the dining room table. "Look at these. Eli painted both of them, with a bit of supervision from Barney."

Alex held them in his hand, staring at two paintings both set in different paddocks on his farm. The first one was of his best broodmare, Black Eliza, her shiny coat depicted perfectly, the shape of her face detailed as she stared down at a new foal. The second one was of three horses running freely across the paddock next to Charlotte's house. In the background were her house, the tree, and the cubbyhouse. They all stared more closely.

Isla reached up and pointed. "Look there's my feet and Charlotte's feet hanging over the edge of the floor."

They laughed and Alex shook his head. "My goodness, you have some talent. I knew Barney could draw and paint but it looks like you can also, Eli. Well done, son. These are beautiful. We should get them framed."

"I'll do you some other ones. I gave these to Charlotte for her birthday last week."

Alex nodded, a bit lost for words.

Charlotte spoke quickly. "Well, Eli. You'll have to do some others for your dad. He could get them framed and hang them on his wall."

Eli thought about that for a while before looking up at his father. "Do you really like them?"

"Of course, I do. I'm serious. They are really good. I used to love drawing. And it's uncanny but I always drew horses. Much like these." He handed the paintings back to Charlotte. "Many years ago, in another life. Actually, I used to do a lot of things." His voice faded away and she could tell he was thinking about the past.

She made her voice sound as cheery as possible. "Okay, you guys. Thanks for having a look. I've kept you longer than I should have."

Her words broke Alex from his reverie. "Thank you for letting us look at these."

"It's lovely to show them to someone. When my brother arrives, I'll get him to hang them for me. Some of these are quite valuable and I want to make sure they're done right."

"I could put them up for you tomorrow if you like." Alex walked up and down in front of them again. "I have the correct hooks and it wouldn't take me long.

Why don't you let me do it for you? A payback for looking after these two so much."

"Yippee," Isla called out. "Does that mean we can come back tomorrow also?"

"If that's okay with Charlotte," he said turning to her. "Barney's in town tomorrow and Belinda-Maree too. The kids would need to come with me. I don't like them at home by themselves."

"I would love that," she said. "It would be great to get these paintings up on the walls. How about mid-morning? I'll make sure to have a pot of tea and some biscuits ready. Miss Isla loves that."

Alex took Isla's hand, who was smiling so hard her face looked like it was going to split. He ruffled her hair. "What do you say, Isla?" he prompted.

She giggled, her words loud and slow. "Everybody got time for that. See ya all tomorrow."

Chapter 9

Alex arrived with the children and Jasper on the dot of ten. The old dog made his way up the back stairs, walking slowly as he came towards Charlotte. When he licked her hand she bent down and scratched the top of his head. He rubbed his body along her leg, before making his way to his position underneath the day bed.

"He's right at home here, isn't he?" Alex smiled at her and her heart missed a beat when he reached over and took her hand in his. He opened her palm. "Here, I have a present for you," he said as he gave her a box of screws and hooks.

She wrapped her fingers around the box. "Thank you." His hand still held hers and she tilted her head on the side and gave him a questioning look.

"Sorry. I'm so sorry. I'm still holding your hand," he muttered.

She giggled. "Yes, you are. It's okay, I have the box."

They stood looking at each other. For once she was lost for words, his eyes drawing her in, his warm touch sending pleasant shivers through her body.

They both jumped, their hands parting and the box falling to the ground as Isla bounded up the stairs, full of energy and trying to beat Eli to the verandah. As usual, she was talking, her words spilling out as she faced her father. "How come you told Belinda that Jasper doesn't like ladies? Just because he growled at her. He loves Charlotte."

"Never mind, Isla," Alex said as he bent down to pick up the hooks which were scattered over the verandah. "I was just trying to make her feel a bit more welcome. It's not my fault he won't go near her without growling."

Charlotte leaned down to give Isla a hug, the little girl responding by wrapping her chubby arms around Charlotte's neck and kissing her on the cheek. "Thank you, Isla. You've made my morning. What a lovely way to start the day!"

Isla took her arms away and jumped up and down, the movement on the verandah boards causing Jasper to open one eye and yap at her. Her voice was shrill and Charlotte could tell she was excited. "Dad's going to hang the pictures and then we're going to have morning tea. Dad brought a packet of biscuits to eat. We can all sit together and we don't have to have morning tea with Lester because he's not invited. And that's the best part. It's just us and no Lester." She put her face up to Charlotte's ear and whispered. "And better still, no Belinda."

Eli stood nearby. "When It's morning teatime, Lester always comes to our house and then we have to sit and be quiet while he talks about the government and all the things they do wrong. Boring."

Alex raised an eyebrow in amusement. "Okay, you

two. Off you go and give us some space. I thought you'd play in the treehouse or out in the yard."

Eli put his hands on his hips and pulled himself up tall. "Actually, Charlotte gets me to help when she does stuff like this. She says she needs someone strong to help." He frowned and looked to her for support.

Alex gazed from one to the other. "Oh, I see. That sounds like a great idea. Maybe today you could assist me."

Eli's face broke into a wide smile, his eyes wide. "I could help you. I can pass you the nails and tell you if the picture is straight."

"That would be fabulous if you could help your dad," Charlotte said. "Because I'm in the middle of cooking a stew. I'll leave it up to you Eli to make sure the pictures go where they should. All I ask is that last one, the one you said was angry, well, please don't put that up. You can stack it down in the laundry for me."

It took a while for Alex and Eli to work out where to position the pictures. A contented feeling filled Charlotte as she worked in the kitchen, listening to Isla chatter nonstop as she helped prepare the stew. The sound of the other two discussing where to put everything was a lively noise in the background. Since she had moved in it had only been her and occasionally the children in the house. She was getting used to the silence, but today it was lovely to hear other voices filling the rooms.

Eli called out from the doorway. "We think we've got it. Dad said can you please come and check and see what you think."

Charlotte lifted Isla down from the kitchen bench where she'd sat with her legs swinging while she peeled carrots before passing them to Charlotte to cut up.

The two of them followed Eli. The paintings leaned against the wall, underneath where they were going to go. She stood next to Alex as he explained the positions, checking with Eli as he went. "We thought you could move this sideboard a little to the left and then these three will fit nicely across this wall. Eli made that suggestion and I think it would work."

She helped Alex move the large sideboard, repositioning a timber box sitting in the middle of it. "I keep all my precious mementos in there. Probably things I should throw out but can't. My dad made it for me," she nodded at Eli, "I would have been about your age and it has always been one of my most treasured possessions."

Isla started talking fast, pulling on her father's hand to make sure she had his full attention. "Charlotte has cards from all the kids she taught. You should read them, Dad. She must be the best teacher in the world. I wish she was my teacher. I don't like Miss Everingham-White."

Alex held his hand up. "Okay, I know. You've told me a million times already. When the term starts up I'll talk to the school and see what we can do."

Isla screwed her face up, her hands on her hips. "I don't want to go back to that school. I want to go to the one here in Bindarra Creek."

"Not now Isla. This isn't the time to discuss that. We need to sort these paintings out."

Eli pulled a piece of paper that was attached by sticky tape to the back of a beautiful landscape. "Someone's left a note," he said. "Do you want me to read it out?"

Charlotte was surprised. She hadn't noticed anything on the back before, but the paintings had been stacked together since arriving from Lucille's. She was intrigued. "Yes, read it out."

He held it in his hand, his eyes roving over it. "It's from your Aunt Lucille. It says, from Lucille, at the bottom. "To my dear Charlie. If you're reading this, then I am probably no longer here. All I have to say is thank goodness you left that dick…head," Eli read the last word in two syllables and took a step back as Charlotte held her hand out for the note. "Bimbo can have him, you deserve so much more and I know you will find someone…"

Charlotte felt her face burn and she took the note from Eli, blinking in shock at the message in the letter. She had rung her aunt a couple of weeks before she passed and Aunt Lucille was delighted that her Charlie, as she called her, had rid herself of Hugh, who she had never liked.

"Who is dick…head?" Isla asked, her big eyes looking up at Charlotte.

Alex chuckled, a glimmer of laughter in his eyes. "Never mind. Let's get on with these paintings." He winked at Charlotte, and she could tell he was trying not to laugh.

The tension left her body and she breathed a heavy sigh. "It's a long story, Now let's get these pictures up. Those spots will be perfect." She folded the note and placed it into the timber box. She must remember to read the rest of it later, but if she knew Aunt Lucille, it probably didn't say too much more than that. She wasn't a sentimental person, instead her words were usually to the point and abrupt. She'd had her say and obviously knew that one day Charlotte would hang the pictures and find her note.

She passed Alex another small painting. It was one she'd done herself and the smoky colours were brushed onto an old piece of timber. The waves of the ocean seemed to leap out from the rough texture of the wood, the puffy clouds with bruised bases looking like they would blow right off the edge. It was a small picture and she looked at it fondly. It was where her parents had always taken her and Jacob for holidays. A deserted beach on North Stradbroke Island. A place where they roamed freely, watched baby turtles hatch from underneath the sand by the light of a full moon, and scurry into the ocean. A couple of them had needed a helping hand, their little legs and tail waving wildly as they searched for the water. In the afternoons and early mornings, dolphins danced in the surf, and further out huge whales travelled north on their way to birth their young, their spouts shooting up and even sometimes their enormous bodies breaching high out of the water.

She looked for a long time at the painting.

"Good memories?" Alex asked.

She held it out for him. "I painted this when I was a teenager. It's where we went for all our childhood holidays. Just Jacob and I, Mum and Dad. I was lucky to grow up in a loving family. The four of us were, and still are very close."

His dark eyes looked into hers, and she was drawn in by his handsome face and the way he moved his fingers through his hair. His white T-shirt moulded his muscled chest, and she tried not to stare at his tanned arms as he held the paintings in place. He'd taken his shoes off before coming in the house and she liked seeing him looking relaxed.

A glimmer of concern crept over his face. "Do you

think I'll be close to my two? It worries me that they're growing up so fast. Sometimes, well most of the time, I don't feel like I'm doing a good job. I've realised lately how much I'm missing out on."

They both looked towards Eli and Isla who had pulled all her old music records out and were going through them.

She kept her voice low. "They do sometimes mention that you don't spend much time with them. I don't mean to criticise, but you did ask. Maybe you should loosen up a bit and have some fun with them. They like it when you do these sorts of things with them. It doesn't have to be anything major. It's the simple things they like."

"I was thinking of flying them and Belinda-Maree down to Sydney. You know we could visit the zoo, the Opera House, catch the ferry across the harbour." He looked over at them, Isla lying on her back, reading the back of a Bryan Ferry cover and Eli, trying to work out how to put a record on the record player. "Then again, maybe I should just take them bushwalking around here, just the three of us."

"Why don't you take them down to the creek crossing? Down behind the stand of fir trees. We all walked there the other day and they wanted to go swimming. Of course, I didn't let them because I hadn't asked you first."

His face lit up and he smiled. "Why don't you come with us. They would love that. They, um, well they don't seem to have much fun with Belinda-Maree."

Isla came up behind him. "Why do we have to call her Belinda-Maree. I'm just going to call her Belinda. I don't care if she gets cranky with me. It's stupid to have two names."

Charlotte went to help Eli try and get the record player to work. They took it apart and cleaned some parts before putting it all back together. She listened to Alex as he explained why it was important to respect a person's name. The conversation flowed between the four of them, now and again a burst of laughter when one of the children said something funny.

It was a cosy atmosphere and almost as if the walls of the house were breathing a sigh of relief to have the sound of happiness between them. It reminded her of times when she was a child and Dad had sat with her playing each one of his records. Her favourite song echoed throughout the room and as the children started dancing she looked up at her paintings now hanging on the wall, a sense of calm and happiness filling her. Her gaze turned to Alex, a feeling of regret that he had a partner. She had to admit, her attraction to him was becoming stronger every time she saw him.

Chapter 10

The morning had been a success and all her paintings were now hanging on the wall. The record player was fixed and now in good working condition. It was time for morning tea and Eli and Isla took their drinks and food up into the cubbyhouse. They were annoyed she didn't join them but she didn't want to be far away from the kitchen, plus as she said, the four of them couldn't all fit up there.

"I'm hopeless at cooking," she said to Alex, "It will be a miracle if that stew tastes any good."

He poured her a cup of tea, passing the plate of biscuits towards her. "I haven't eaten Iced Vos Vos since I was a child. This place is like a kid's paradise."

"They're a tradition in our family." She dunked her biscuit in her tea, laughing when he tentatively followed and did the same. His laugh was deep and infectious, and he continued to dunk the biscuit and then eat it until it was all gone.

Taking a seat at the top of the stairs, he tried to cajole Jasper out of the shady spot where he was sleeping. "Poor old thing. Lester wants me to take him to the vet and get him put down but I don't have the heart to. The kids would be so upset."

"We had a dog like that and it lived for years, partially deaf and blind. Jasper isn't in any pain and still manages to walk over here with the kids. He seems happy enough."

"I'm glad you said that, because that's what I think, but everyone else disagrees and I feel like I'm losing the battle. Belinda can't stand the sight of him, she shudders every time he comes her way. He's been with us for so long and I know Isla sneaks him in at night and lets him into her bedroom to sleep. Belinda-Maree would have a fit if she knew."

"Your Isla is a bright button. So is Eli. Not much gets past them. They'd told me that Lester doesn't like the dog."

He sighed and looked across the paddocks towards his house. "Lester, bloody Lester. He's a bit of a thorn in my side." He turned back to her, his eyes narrowing. "Can I tell you something confidential?"

"Sure," she replied. "I don't repeat anything I'm told."

"Lester arrived on the scene only a couple of years ago. He drifted into Bindarra Creek and somehow met up with Bridie, my sister. She'd been single for years and lived in the cottage when we were here. I've got a place in Sydney as well and we used to go back and forth to here, when it fitted in with the kids."

He stretched his legs out. "I know the locals in town think I won't hang around, but my plans are to live here full-time. I'm not sure if that's what Belinda wants though."

Charlotte raised her eyebrows.

He took a long sip of his tea, patting the top of Jasper's head who lay next to him. "Anyway, getting back to what I wanted to talk about. When Lester moved in with Bridie I wasn't that happy about it, but she'd done a lot for me after the kid's mother left and I'm not sure how I would have coped without her. I mean, Bridie's not loved like you are by the kids. It's amazing how quickly they've become attached to you. She doesn't cuddle them and they don't tell her things or talk in-depth with her. But she cleaned, cooked, and looked after all the bills, schooling, and everything they needed. I couldn't say no to him being there."

"That would have been hard. I've only met your sister once and she seems like a nice person."

"She is, but I feel like she's picked the wrong bloke. She was stripped of any confidence after her first marriage broke up. He wasn't a particularly pleasant person either and didn't let her have a say in anything. You would have thought she'd have learnt from that. She's gone for the same type of person. Lester rules the roost! I have to bite my tongue sometimes. She's a grown woman and it's not my place to interfere. They aren't married but he acts as if they are and refers to her as his wife. He was okay at the start, actually, he was a pain because he was so nice. He's nasty to the kids sometimes when he thinks Barney or I aren't watching. That's also one of the reasons I like them away at school and not here with him. I don't trust him."

"They told me you said not to be near him by them-selves." She crossed her legs and straightened her blouse, tying her hair up in a messy bun on top of her head. "It's funny that you say that about him because I've only met Lester a couple of times but I get a strange feeling about him. I think I know him from somewhere but I can't quite place where."

"Where would you know him from?"

"I don't know but it's been niggling me. Maybe it's my imagination."

Alex stood up and came to sit beside her, his bare feet touching hers as he stretched out his legs. "Oh, sorry. I wasn't playing footsy with you." They both laughed and pulled their legs in. Their eyes met and dropped and she could feel the heat in her face.

"It's okay," she said.

He looked up at her and she tried to read the look on his face. Was it confusion, affection or just the friendly look of a neighbour whose foot happened to touch hers? For a moment she thought about putting her foot back on top of his and seeing what his reaction was.

Ridiculous she told herself again. *Neighbours, friends, that was it!*

For a moment neither spoke and she regained her composure as they both waved at Isla who was hanging upside down by her legs on a sturdy branch. "Okay," Alex said, suddenly sitting upright. "I won't panic. Does she normally do that?"

"She's fine. Didn't you used to do that as a kid?"

"I did. I grew up on a horse property not far from here. I had Bridie and two brothers to play with and we were all as wild as each other. I don't know when or where I lost that free thinking."

"I told you. Don't think like an old person. You'll lose the fun in life."

He leaned towards her, his eyes intent. "So, tell me then. Who is dickhead, and who is Bimbo?"

Chapter 11

Whcn Alex leaned towards Charlotte he had to resist reaching up and touching her hair. What was it that made him want to be close to her? He pulled himself into line; these feelings were totally inappropriate. He'd only just met her and more importantly, he was engaged. Engaged to a beautiful woman who adored him. Belinda-Maree. Even thinking about her made him feel guilty. It was *not* okay to have feelings for another woman. There were so many good qualities to his fiancée, but, lately he was seeing another side of her, particularly when the kids were around.

Their relationship had often been long distance which had worked well to start with. They had different careers and he would never stop Belinda-Maree from aiming for the top in her acting career. That profession did take her away for long periods of time though, and sometimes he'd questioned if the relationship was going to work in the long-term. Would they always spend lengthy periods away from each other?

Now as he watched Charlotte as she tried to avoid

his questions about her aunt's note he realised how different she was to Belinda-Maree; she was the opposite. There was a freshness to her personality, a natural affection towards the children and just a calm, beautiful poise in the way she talked and interacted with him. It was hard to drag his gaze away from her face, those intense green eyes and gorgeous wavy hair. Hair that he wanted to run his fingers through.

His conscience bothered him. Charlotte was his neighbour and a friend. He needed to go back home, gather his thoughts and focus on the woman he was engaged to.

Standing up he started collecting the cups. "C'mon you two. It's time to go home," he called out, watching carefully as both Isla and Eli swung down from the tree-house. "No wonder these kids love it here," he remarked to Charlotte, looking down at Isla's and Eli's dusty feet and clothes.

Today they'd each talked about a lot of things in their past. The strange thing was that even though he'd only known Charlotte for a short time there was an instant familiarity, a friendship between the two of them. The trouble was, if he was honest, there was a whole lot more of feeling there than just that. Intimacy, longing, tenderness?

Did he feel that with Belinda-Maree?

He cleared his throat. "I'll see you soon, Charlotte. Thanks."

She'd smiled at him but hadn't answered.

Chapter 12

A multitude of thoughts filled Charlotte's mind as Alex drove away. She waved them off, both kids hanging out the car windows along with Jasper who pushed his nose into the wind, making it look like there was a smile stretched across his furry face.

Today they'd had a long conversation without Eli and Isla listening. He'd confided his worries about the kids and his relationship with them as well as the issue of keeping Belinda-Maree happy. It sounded like she was high-maintenance and not someone who wanted to have an instant family that included a six and eight-year-old.

"You'll work it out, I guess," she'd said, careful not to say too much of what she was thinking.

The house was quiet without them and Charlotte put on another record to have some background noise as she cleaned up the kitchen. It had been fun to talk about art and music with Alex. He had the same tastes she did and he'd confided in her that he'd hidden his old records. Belinda-Maree didn't like what he did and said records were old-school and only fit for the bin. All she did was complain when he put them on and it was easier to give in rather than cause an argument. She also didn't like him being barefoot outside the house and he commented how enjoyable the day had been without wearing shoes.

She made herself another cup of tea, sipping it slowly as she walked up and down in front of the newly hung paintings. Fancy Aunt Lucille leaving that note and how funny that Eli had read it out. It was good to talk to someone about her broken marriage and Alex had been sympathetic and told her she was better off without Hugh. His first marriage had been similar, except his wife had taken off and left two small children behind. Not that he minded her being completely out of the picture, he'd said. The way she'd behaved and her disregard for the kids was unforgivable. Such a long time had passed since she left, that the kids no longer asked about her and they'd all got used to her having no contact with them.

Charlotte tidied some of the ornaments and re-arranged other smaller pieces of furniture. The room was warm and imbued with a sense of creativity, the paintings adding that extra element she wanted for when she opened as a retreat. That was what she needed to do for the next couple of weeks before Jacob arrived. Concentrate on the cabins and start cleaning them out. That would keep her busy and stop her thinking about Alex.

Today he hadn't sounded sure about his long-term plans with Belinda-Maree. It was as if he'd wanted to offload on her, to get some advice. Her stomach fluttered when she thought about his eyes gazing into hers and how close they'd been when he leaned in. There was something about him that made her want to spend more time with him. She needed to be careful though, he was already taken. If what she was feeling lingered, she'd need to remember she was just a friend and nothing more.

———

ISLA AND ELI appeared regularly each morning, Isla's chatter audible long before the two of them reached Charlotte's house. She was surprised early one morning when Alex arrived with them, Jasper as usual trailing along behind. Alex wore boardshorts and an old T-shirt, the kids were dressed in swimmers with towels draped over their shoulders.

"It's hot today and we're going down to the creek crossing. We'd love it if you came with us?" he asked. "Belinda-Maree has gone to Sydney for a few days for work so it's just the three of us."

Isla piped up. "Just the three of us. Belinda is always going away." She went to say more but Alex frowned at her and she took the cue to be quiet.

It was always just the three of them, Charlotte thought as she stopped sweeping, the dust flying through the air, covering Jasper as he walked up to her. Bending down she stroked his head, his old eyes looking up at her, as he nuzzled his nose into her hand. He lay at her feet, exhausted from the walk.

She straightened up, looking directly into Alex's eyes. She knew she must look a mess, her hair tied back loosely; in her usual cleaning clothes: an old dirty pair of denim shorts and a stained singlet. His eyes roamed over her body and her skin tingled under his gaze.

"I wasn't expecting anyone," she tried to push her hair back from her face. "I've been cleaning. I look terrible."

A wide smile crossed his face. "You could never look terrible. Gorgeous as always."

Her face burned and she turned away quickly. "Give me a minute. Yes, I'd love to come."

Although it was winter, today felt like a summer's day. The regular rain had skirted their properties and although there had been a couple of downpours, they were waiting for the winter storms. A swim would wash the dust away and revitalise her.

When she walked back out, the three of them were sitting on the stairs, Jasper lying at their feet. She stopped and listened to Alex who was telling a story about when he was a kid and one of his mares needed help having a foal.

His relationship with the kids was improving every time she saw him. Her stomach did a strange little flip as he stopped talking and looked up at her.

A pair of shorts covered the bottom half of her bathers and she was pleased her legs were tanned from the time she'd spent outside. She slipped a pair of thongs on. "Right, ready to go?"

He shook his head but his eyes never left hers. "You look, um, you look, jeez, ready to go for a swim."

She laughed at him and flicked her towel at his legs, amused to see that he also had resorted to wearing old thongs. No doubt the footwear had been taken out of hiding and concealed from the beady eyes of Belinda.

Winding tracks that horses and cattle had followed

over the years, curled their way down towards the western reaches of Charlotte's property. Alex and Eli led the way while Isla and Charlotte followed, the two of them continually stopping to pick wildflowers or to look at interesting rocks they spotted along the way.

Apart from the night Charlotte had arrived, August had been a dry month and everyone was waiting for the rain, not only to re-fill the dams and help the grass grow but to dampen the dust that seemed to filter through every part of the house and cover the cars and washing on the line. They passed through a gate, Alex lecturing the children that they were never to pass through here without him or Charlotte. They waited while he shut it, all watching patiently until Jasper also passed through. The old dog seemed to have gained some energy and although his pace was slow and they stopped a few times to wait for him, he kept walking.

Isla skipped ahead and Eli jogged to keep up with her, the two of them laughing and talking as they went. Charlotte breathed in deeply, the golden colours of the sun filtering across the long grass in the paddocks.

In the distance ragged hills bordered the horizon, puffy white clouds sitting high above them. The area was part of the Akuna National Park, its walking tracks and climbing ridges popular with hikers and campers. The area closest to Charlotte's property however was remote and cut off from the more popular sites.

Alex looked towards the mountains. "No one goes through those parts anymore. There were a few rock-slides many years ago that blocked some of the trails. The entire area has been abandoned for years. There hasn't even been a good fire through there for a long time." He pointed to one of the higher peaks. "They say the bushrangers used to hide out in some of the caves. You can see why. No one would ever be able to get to them."

The bush was dense on the sides of the mountain and steep ravines cut through the slopes, the vegetation darker and thicker where water flowed down from the peaks. Looking towards the mountains, she shaded her eyes. "It doesn't seem that far from here. I'll have to go for a walk that way, once I'm a bit more organised."

"Just take care. The area is thick with black snakes and it's easy to get lost in there. The tracks are over-grown. Let me know if you go with your brother and I'll come for a hike."

"I'd like that, she replied. "I need to get Jacob interested in the place. I'd love it if he'd move down and live here with me. He needs a change in his life." They continued talking until they reached the creek, the banks lined with weeping gums and other small trees. A flock of galahs took off from the shelter of hanging branches, their squawks echoing across the plains that stretched out to the south. Alex and Eli walked in front, following a track that ran alongside the side of the creek while Charlotte and Isla waited for Jasper to catch up.

Chapter 13

Isla grabbed Charlotte's hand, swinging it back and forth. Charlotte knew that Isla would be brimming with happiness spending a day with Alex.

She squeezed her hand. "It's a lovely day, Isla."

Isla grinned back at her. "I have a secret to tell you. Quick, while Dad and Eli can't hear."

Charlotte bent down and Isla stood on her tiptoes, checking to make sure no one else was listening. "Eli and I follow Lester this far sometimes. We have to hide behind the bushes so he doesn't see us. He never has though."

Taken aback, Charlotte squatted down beside her. "What? What do you mean you follow him? Does he come down here for a swim?"

Isla cupped her hand around Charlotte's ear. "It's a really big secret. You can't tell anyone."

Charlotte waited for her to continue, an uneasiness settling in the pit of her stomach. "I know a secret that no one else knows. I bet you don't know where he goes. He goes between the big boulders further behind the creek. There are caves in there. Barney said the bushrangers from the olden days used to live there. The police couldn't find them."

Her body tensed at the thought of the two of them alone with Lester. "You're not allowed out this far by yourselves. I don't want you following him again. Promise me you won't come through that gate by yourselves. Your father has said that you aren't allowed to go out there without him."

Isla scrunched her face up, her eyes narrowing. Obviously, she'd thought Charlotte would be perfect to add to their spying and conspiracy adventures, but now she didn't seem so sure. "We never go further than the shed there." She pointed to a fallen down building, its roof and walls crumbling and barely visible behind a rambling bougainvillea bush, the pink flowers vivid amidst the dryness of the paddock. "You can hide behind it or get inside and he can't see you."

Charlotte put on the sternest look she could muster. "There could be snakes in there. Promise me you won't go there again."

Isla twisted her mouth and tried to change the topic away from promises. "We don't know why he goes up there. He walks really fast and we never see him come back. We get bored of waiting."

A shiver ran down Charlotte's spine and she peered around in case Lester was behind them now. Surely he would have seen the kids following him. He wasn't that stupid. More the question though, why was he coming out this way and cutting through her property? She grabbed Isla's hand so they could walk faster. "C'mon, let's catch up with the others."

Charlotte mulled over what Isla had told her, trying

to act like there was nothing wrong, but the thought of them following Lester made her skin prickle with fear. Alex had been adamant they weren't to be with him by themselves, and alone in a paddock, far from home, was even a worse scenario. As soon as she got a chance she would let him know and he could talk to them. Once he knew about it and disciplined them they wouldn't go again. He could be quite stern when he put on his serious voice.

Alex and Eli were already in the water by the time Charlotte arrived with Isla and Jasper in tow. The creek was flowing nicely due to earlier rain further up the hills and was perfect for swimming. Even in the driest months, the rock pool managed to hold a decent amount of water. She helped Isla get out of her dress, giggling with her as it got stuck, wrestling it back and forth over her head until she was freed. Charlotte stepped out of her shorts, thankful that her body was well-toned and that she still looked fit. It was amazing that she did, because other than walking around the paddocks she didn't do any other regular exercise. "Good genes," Aunt Lucille used to say, her legs still long and slim into her later years.

The water was icy cold but Charlotte slid into it, the water streaming from her hair as she popped back up. A loud yell from Alex and Eli made her laugh as they both jumped into the water. She kept moving so she wouldn't feel the cold so much and waded back near the bank, holding out her arms for Isla who was hesitant to enter. Alex came up beside her, talking to Isla and reminding her about the depths of creeks and how not to dive into them until you knew how deep they were and if there were any submerged logs or rocks beneath the water.

"You have to test it out first," Eli added. "Otherwise you'll break your neck if you dive in. Never jump in without testing it out first."

"That's right, Alex grinned at him. "You do listen to what I say."

"Charlotte and Barney told us that too."

Alex nodded and rolled his eyes. "Okay, I get it. You're lucky you've got so many people looking out for you."

Soon they were all floating around in the pool. Isla took a while to perfect floating on her back and Charlotte told her that perhaps if she didn't keep talking she might be able to concentrate on staying horizontal. Silence soon fell, the only sound the noise of the creek as it tumbled over the boulders near them. Sunlight filtered in through the trees, and Charlotte closed her eyes, soaking in the quiet, her legs stretched out, the water lapping around her body a fresh clean feeling.

Suddenly she screamed as something grabbed her feet. A clenching firm grip that squeezed tightly. She struggled and tried to stand upright, glaring hard at Eli and Alex who swam near her, laughing as they repeated their actions on Isla. The pool erupted into a splashing squealing melee as the girls grouped together, splashing with all their might at the foot-grabbers.

The tranquillity disappeared and the rest of the time was spent watching the kids swing from a rope high on the bank into the deepest part of the pool. She'd laughed and splashed around, waving her hands in the air to encourage Isla and cheering loudly along with Alex at the antics of the children.

Afterwards, they sat on the bank, munching on cookies and sipping cold drinks they'd brought with them. The children went back into the pool, racing each other from one side to the other and seeing who could float on their back the longest.

She sat next to Alex, their legs dangling over the edge of the rock pool, the cool water refreshing on her feet. He swatted a horsefly that landed on her arm.

"Maybe there's rain coming," he said, flicking the dead fly in the pool. Dragonflies buzzed over the top of the water, and a kookaburra perched on a branch near them peered down, its head moving from side to side, taking in the action.

Alex turned to her. He'd thrown a T-shirt on when he'd got out of the pool but she couldn't help but notice his muscular chest as he'd stood up to his hips in the water. His shoulders were broad and his body fit and well-defined. No wonder he and Belinda had graced the social pages of the newspapers down south. They made a striking good-looking couple. His hair had started to dry and small curls covered the top of his head. God only knows what hers looked like, Charlotte thought as she tried to push the thick tresses back behind her ears. She leaned back, lying backward so she could grab a hair tie from the backpack she had brought with her. She could feel his eyes on her as her body stretched backward, the black one-piece clinging to her body. Sitting up, she tied her hair up, curling her hair slowly around her hands, moving slowly to emphasise her actions.

When she turned to him, he looked away, but she knew he had been watching her. What was he thinking? What did it matter if he liked the way she looked? He lived in a world far different from her own. Don't even think like that, she cautioned herself.

His gaze turned back to the pool, both children sitting on the opposite bank, chatting and looking for treasures in the mud.

"They have been getting on so well lately," he said. "I don't know what you've done with them but they're like different kids."

She pulled her legs out of the water and hugged her knees. "I haven't done anything. They just needed a bit of attention and freedom."

He looked at her. "Thank you. And I mean it. I've come to realise so much over the last couple of weeks and it's all thanks to you."

She blushed. "Oh no. I haven't done anything. Besides, you already have your life in order. You have your property, your horses, and your family." She wanted to add, "and of course, you have an amazing, beautiful, model and actress fiancée."

But she didn't.

"I do. But do you know what? Today and some of the other times I've spent with you has made me happier than anything I've done in a long time." He stopped talking and watched the children.

"It's the simple things. I keep saying it."

He scowled and splashed the water with his foot. "I'm not sure at the moment what I want."

"You're talking to the wrong person here. Don't ask me about what makes someone happy. I've stuffed up ten years of my life. I think you need to talk to someone who has their life together."

The surface of the water glimmered in the speckled sunlight, its surface broken by the awkward swimming motions of Isla who was thrashing her way towards them. When she got halfway she stopped. "I can't swim any further. Dad can you come and get me."

Charlotte put her hand on Alex's arm to stop him as he went to get in the water. "Make her come here herself. She's got to learn to push herself and not take the easy way out.

He sat back down. "Keep going. You're a good swimmer. You can do it."

"What if I drown?"

"You won't. Come on."

Isla put her head down and kicked her legs, her arms moving quicker when she noticed Eli coming up from behind her. When she reached where Charlotte's legs dangled in the water she grabbed Charlotte's feet, bouncing up and down as Charlotte raised them in the air before splashing them back down in the water. Before long they were all back in having a final swim. Alex was quiet, a thoughtful look on his face. She found herself taking sneaky glimpses of him as he threw Isla up and down in the air. He had a lovely kind nature and now he was relaxing more around the kids, she saw a different side to him. She forced herself to look away. Whatever these feelings were she was developing towards him, they needed to stop.

He was a friend. A neighbour who confided in her and asked for advice. That was all. He had his own wonderful life, his future years set in place.

———

AS THEY WALKED BACK through the paddocks Charlotte trailed behind, waiting for Jasper who walked for a bit, but then sat down to take a rest. A tree offered him shade and she sat with him for a while, the old dog lying down and taking a short nap while she rested with him. Alex made his way back to her. "I told the kids to wait at your place for us. I thought this old fella would be trailing behind."

She patted Jasper's head. "He's okay. Just having a little shuteye. Actually, I'm glad you're here. I wanted to tell you something Isla told me on the way here."

By the time she finished telling Alex the story about the kids following Lester across the paddocks, Jasper had woken and started walking. They followed behind him. Alex was upset.

"I wish I could tell Lester to leave but I don't want to upset Bridie. I owe her for all the help she's given me. She's not a bad person but I'm sure she's been drawn to him because someone finally paid her some attention."

Charlotte was worried too. "Nothing is more important than the safety of your kids, but I do understand your dilemma."

He looked at her, their eyes meeting and holding. "I'll have another talk to them about where they can and can't go. I won't mention that you said anything. Barney is usually two steps behind them and they keep busy at your place. Hopefully they won't go down there again without either of us. Eli mentioned something to me once before. It's interesting he's heading out that way."

"Yes, he doesn't seem like the bushwalking type."

Alex ran his hand through his hair. "I'm interested what he's up to. We'll have to keep an eye on him."

—

CHARLOTTE HADN'T SEEN Alex or the children for a few days when she received a surprise phone call from Belinda-Maree. "Hello Charlotte. I've arrived back from Sydney and you wouldn't be aware of it, but it's Alex's birthday on Saturday. I'm throwing him a party. People are driving up from Sydney and caterers are organised. If you could be there at two in the afternoon, I'm sure Alex would love to see you there."

Belinda had accentuated her last sentence, sarcasm dripping from her words. Her manner confused Charlotte and she couldn't think quick enough to make up an excuse. It was difficult to lie when everyone knew she rarely went anywhere or had anyone come to stay. If only it had been in a few weeks. Her first guests for the cabins were coming and that would have been a perfect excuse. She tried to sound enthusiastic. "Of course, Belinda. I'd love to come."

There was a hint of annoyance in Belinda's voice when she replied. "You weren't on my list but Alex insisted that I ring you. Some of the locals are coming, but that table is full. There's a seating plan and I'll put you with Barney and that lot. Oh, and also, Charlotte, if you don't mind, please remember my name. It's Belinda-Maree."

"Sorry. Yes of course. What time again?"

Charlotte hung up feeling like she hadn't been given a choice. The conversation hadn't been an invitation or a question, rather a demand to attend. She had also detected a nasty tone in Belinda's conversation.

She sighed. What on earth was she going to wear and what do you buy a man for his fortieth birthday?

A man that she cared way too much for.

A man she should stay away from.

Chapter 14

The day was a typical cloudless August day; the perfect day for a party. Barney was going to come and pick Charlotte up. That way she could have a few drinks and not worry about walking home through the paddocks after dark. She didn't intend staying late anyway. She'd make an appearance, mingle for a respectful time and then come home.

She stood in front of the mirror, super critical of how she looked. Why was the thought of how she looked making her nervous?

The party was going to be outside under a large marquee so she could only hope the dress she wore would be suitable. This was the jet-setting polo crowd though and then there would also be some of Belinda's posh friends from the TV industry attending.

Isla had kept her up to date with all the arrangements. Belinda had bought Isla a new dress and shoes and as Isla repeated, using over-dramatic words and actions, "Dad and Belinda had a very big fight. Not like the usual arguments that they have, this one was a really

really, really, huge one. It was all because Belinda got me make-up from the shop in town and a straightener for my hair."

Charlotte tried to keep a straight face as Isla continued in the most grown-up voice she could muster. "Dad came in when she was practising on me. I was cranky anyway because she made me sit still for a really long time while she put that hot thing on my hair. It hurt when she pulled it through it. She didn't make Eli use that hot straightener thing so why should I. She said I wasn't allowed to come to Dad's party unless I did what she said."

Charlotte couldn't help herself, intrigued by the story. "Oh dear. What happened next?"

Isla's eyes widened. "Dad picked up all the makeup and threw it in the bin. He went crazy at her and took the straightener thing and put it in the bin too. She yelled back at him and told him, what would he know and that he was turning us into country pumpkins."

Charlotte corrected her. "Bumpkins?"

"Yes, that's what she said, country bumpkins. I didn't know what that was but it must be bad because Dad got even angrier and told her she was never to buy me stuff like that again. He said she had to take the dress back to the shop. He said it made me look like something, I can't remember the word. I didn't like the dress anyway but I was cranky he made her take the shoes back too. I liked them. They had big heels and made me a lot taller."

"Oh dear. So, what are you going to wear now?"

"I have lots of other dresses. Dad said I can just wear one of them and he told me I can wear my riding boots if I want. The party is outside on the grass and he said there's no need to get all fizzy up about it."

"Maybe tizzied up, or fussy?"

"Yes, that's what he said. Anyway, they aren't talking and Dad slept in the other room which I like because I went in and slept with him in the morning. He never sleeps in normally because she makes him get up and…"

Charlotte put her hand up. "Okay, I think I have the story. I'm sure you'll look lovely at the party. You can come and talk to me because I won't know anyone."

Now as she turned around in front of the mirror Charlotte thought about the information Isla had shared. No doubt Alex and Belinda had kissed and made up. It was usual for couples to argue. She flattened her eyebrows, trying to push them up in the middle. It had been one of the best parts of moving to Bindarra Creek. She hadn't had to worry about facials, hair-dressers, or beauticians since she'd arrived. Those days were long gone and if people didn't like the natural way she looked then that was their problem. A light smattering of makeup smoothed any lines on her face and she'd even applied a gloss to her lips. Done, she thought. She'd settled on an elegant knee-length dress. The fabric was soft and clung nicely to her body, accentuating her slim waist and legs. Boots and a thick warm jacket would be best for the outside occasion and finished off her outfit nicely.

Her hair as usual was thick and bouncy, a clip holding back one side, the waves spiralling down past her shoulders. Green eyes peered back at her and she looked hard at herself. She looked alright, well anyway, this was as good as it was going to get. Dressing up and mingling with the rich and famous didn't concern her, but on the other hand, it also didn't interest her.

Barney arrived on time, waving at her from the driver's seat as she walked out to the car.

"Woo Hoo," he said. "Don't you look mighty fine all dressed up."

She settled herself into the front seat next to him. "Thanks, Barney. I don't go out much these days." She looked him up and down. "You look pretty good yourself."

Barney wore long pants and a collared shirt, his shiny leather boots finishing off his outfit. "You don't get me in these very often. I think the last time I wore them was Mavis's funeral."

***

The back yard of Bentley Estate was set up with white chairs and tables covered in crisp white linen tablecloths. The area was shaded by a large marquee, a huge chandelier hanging from the middle. Large potted plants were scattered throughout and smaller silver tables were decorated with massive vases filled with roses. Charlotte was riveted by the flowers and couldn't help but think about how much so many beautiful roses would cost, not to mention the elaborate decorations that hung from the ceiling and edges of the marquee.

Caterers served fancy nibblies on large silver trays and waiters in formal dress flounced around ensuring everyone's glasses were filled. There would have been a hundred or more people attending and Charlotte was glad she had worn the outfit she had on, her dress perfect for the occasion. Isla squealed and ran to her when she arrived. "Look, Dad said to wear these and they're just like yours. She pointed to her leather boots.

"They're old, but they keep my feet clean for now. Yours are beautiful. They look new."

Charlotte cuddled her arms around Isla, squeezing her tightly. "You look lovely, Isla and your father is right with his choice of shoes. Beautiful!" Isla stepped back when Charlotte let go of her, twirling excitedly to show off her dress. "This one is old but it's my favourite. Look at the yellow flowers on it."

"It's perfect, and I love the flowers. I had a dress just like that when I was a little girl."

Isla beamed as she took Charlotte's hand, leading her over to the area where people were mingling in crowds. Alex spotted them and made his way towards them. His dark eyes settled on hers and his smile swept over her, the genuinely warm welcome a relief in amongst the crowd of strangers.

He swung Isla up into his arms, her little arms wrapping around his neck. "Thanks so much for coming, Charlotte," he said. "You look lovely."

Her heart fluttered wildly as their eyes met and she took a deep breath. "Happy birthday," she said as she handed him a small gift, wrapped in one of Isla's drawings. Before he had time to reply, Belinda came up behind them, handing Charlotte a glass of champagne before giving her a kiss on each cheek. Her voice was husky, just like an actress's voice, Charlotte thought.

"And this must be the amazing Charlotte. Thanks for coming. It's so lovely to have a neighbour here to celebrate with us." It was the first time Charlotte had met Belinda in person and she was awed by her tall figure and glossy dark hair, not a kink in it as it sat perfectly on her bare shoulders. Charlotte ran her hand over her own hair, flattening it and pushing it back behind her ears.

She tried to stop herself from feeling intimidated by the way Belinda looked but it was difficult not to notice how beautiful she was. She had after all been the advertisement girl for Calron Shampoo and Charlotte could understand why. Her face was perfect, with olive skin and big eyes that flitted around, looking everyone up and down and nodding at those who were standing nearby. Her smile revealed a perfect line of white teeth, her lips thick and covered in dark red lipstick. Charlotte tried not to stare, but Belinda's lips were unnaturally plump, her face not seeming to move when she talked. She wore a tight, very short, emerald, green dress. A plunging neckline revealed a large set of breasts and Charlotte wondered how she kept everything intact and not popping out when her dress was cut so low. She blinked several times, overwhelmed by the diamonds dripping from Belinda's ears and neck. Feeling very much like the country bumpkin, she dragged her eyes away, trying not to stare.

"It's lovely to be asked," she replied, trying to sound as confident and relaxed as she could.

She knew Alex was watching her, his lips curling in a reassuring smile. Did he realise that she felt a little out of her depth? Even before she arrived at Bindarra Creek she'd been tucked away for months, staying at home and keeping to herself. The last couple of weeks most of the socialising she'd done was with Alex, the kids and Barney. Taking another deep breath, she reminded herself that she could do this, appearances meant nothing and in the past her life had involved mixing with all types of people.

Alex opened her present, his hand running over the small painting she had done for him. It was completed in the same style as the one he had admired at her house the day he hung the paintings in her lounge room. This one, however, was of the creek and rock pool where they swam last week. The pool shimmered aqua green, the dark growth bordering it throwing shadows across its surface. The finished product was exactly as she had envisaged, the fun and energy of the day captured in the colours. He ran his fingers across the two children, hanging onto ropes as they swung out across the pool. You could almost hear their squeals and yells as they prepared to plunge into the cold water below.

A whimsical look crossed his face, his voice full of emotion.

"Thank you. You've captured the mood and the beauty of the creek, perfectly."

They stared at each other, both remembering the day, the deep conversations, the advice given and most of all the relaxed and pleasant hours they'd spent together.

Belinda interrupted, taking the painting from him. "Here give me that. It's exquisite. Looks like you did a trip to the big smoke for your birthday shopping. I'll put it with the other presents on the gift table. I'll keep the card with it, that way Alex will remember who gave him what." With that she flounced off, leaving the two of them staring at each other.

"It was a fun day," she said. "You have a lot of friends here today. The marquee looks beautiful."

He cast his eyes around the crowd, a variety of ages and different people. "It's a bit fancy for me, but it does look nice. Most of the guests are only acquaintances, business connections." He nodded to a group of women, all around the same age. "They're Belinda's crew from her work. They are all from the world of movies and television. I haven't met half of them."

"Oh. I see a couple of faces there I know from TV. Wow, some of them are quite famous."

"There's also a table full of some of the local people from town. Some couldn't make it because of a fund-raising event at the pub. But you should find a few over there you might know." He bent down and lowered his voice. "To tell you the truth, I'd rather be sitting with them than Belinda's lot.' Shaking his head, he looked straight at her. "We're a world apart at the moment, her and I."

He took a sip from his drink, his other arm still cuddling Isla who laid her head down on his shoulder and closed her eyes. "This little one is worn out already. Such a build-up to the day. She and Eli have been going non-stop all morning."

"I think she just likes snuggling up to you." Charlotte laughed as Isla opened her eyes, looking quickly at her before closing them again.

"There aren't any other kids here for her to play with and famous people don't mean much to my kids. They're all here to mingle with the other famous people. To be *seen*." He shook his head, a hint of mockery in his voice. "It's a completely different life."

His tone changed and her heart ached for him. "Your fiancée has gone to a lot of trouble for your birth-day. Maybe you should look a bit happier and put any arguments aside for the day. You don't look or sound very cheerful."

He straightened up and pulled a funny face.

"Gotcha, Charlie. Thanks for the tip. You sound like you were advising one of the kids. You're right and I do have some close friends here to celebrate with."

Although she'd decided not to drink too much, she tipped her drink up. She was going to need something to get her through the next couple of hours. Her voice was low. "I'll let you get away with the "Charlie" this time. No one, but close family call me that. Now put a smile on your face and have a good time. Well at least try and look like you are."

He tilted his head back, running his hand through his hair, his laughter loud and drawing attention from a group standing next to them. Leaning over, he whispered in her ear. "Thanks. Charlie. I'll talk to you after this is all over."

———

ISLA SNUGGLED into Alex's shoulder as he walked away from Charlotte. His heart thumped hard. It had just come out. He'd called her Charlie and she'd let him get away with it. It was strange seeing her with Belinda-Maree and seeing them side-by-side had accentuated the differences between the two of them. The differences he'd been thinking about for a few weeks.

Charlotte had looked a little nervous and he had really wanted to put his arm around her and tell her she looked stunning. Her dress clung to her body, high-lighting her lithe figure. He'd dragged his eyes away from her legs and the sexiest pair of leather boots he'd ever seen. For a moment his mind wandered and he thought about what it would be like to unzip the boots and slowly remove them. He'd seen her slender feet at the rockpools. What would it be like to massage them?

A small voice brought him back to reality. "Yes, I heard you, Isla. You said Charlotte is your favourite person." Isla snuggled into him. After the dramas of the last couple of days she deserved a cuddle. Yesterday she'd come and found him in the stables. Everyone was driving her crazy and she'd had enough. Once she started it had been impossible to stop her and he'd let her talk. At this stage— of the lead-up to a party that he hadn't really wanted— he wished he also could let his words tumble out. He'd sat Isla on top of the horse he was brushing, trying to keep a serious face as he listened.

"I'm tired of getting dressed up and running around fetching everything for Belinda. She's so bossy and I wish she'd go back to Sydney and leave us all by ourselves. It wouldn't be so bad if she liked me or sat and played with me like Charlotte does. But all she ever does is tell me to be quiet and stop talking so much. Charlotte's my best friend and when I have to go back to school I'll miss her, just as much as I'll miss you, Daddy" She'd stopped for a second and made sure he was listening. "I won't miss Lester though. I think Charlotte told you we followed him. That was my secret. I'm a good detective and he's not nice and he's sneaky."

———

ALEX THOUGHT about Isla's words from yesterday as he turned around. Lester was sitting at a table near to where they were standing, looking at someone in the crowd. He followed Lester's gaze to see what he was looking at.

He was staring straight at Charlotte as she approached the table where some of the guests from town were sitting. A twisted sneer crossed Lester's face and he sat upright, his hand reaching up to play with his earring.

Isla had also noticed and she whispered in his ear. "Lester is looking at Charlotte and that's how he looks at Jasper." She squeezed her father's neck harder and gripped her legs tighter around his waist. "Why does he stare at her like that?"

Alex gritted his teeth. The man was dangerous. That was the first time he'd ever seen him look like that, and at Charlotte. What was his problem?

━━

"WELCOME to the Bindarra Creek table, Charlotte," Hunter Sullivan stood up and pulled a chair out for her. His voice was friendly and familiar and she sighed a breath of relief. "There aren't many of us here yet. Most are coming after the fundraiser in town. This is Chelsea, my wife."

Smiling, she relaxed a little. "Pleased to meet you Chelsea, and hello Jaclyn. It's lovely to see some familiar faces."

Hunter sat back down as he continued to introduce her. "By the looks you already know Jaclyn. Over here you have the rest of the Rossiter mob, Jaclyn's better half, Ryan and his brother Joe. And next to them, Marsha and Chen Wang."

Charlotte turned to the others, holding out her hand to shake theirs across the table. "Pleased to meet you all."

"How have you settled in," Marsha asked. "I love your retreat idea. I paint a little myself. Perhaps when you're up and running I'll treat myself a few days to let my creative talents flow."

"We work from home so she's her own boss," Chen added. He turned to his wife. "I think you'd struggle to get away without Gavin though."

Marsha smiled. "Gavin is our only son. He's thirteen and crazy about horses. Alex has said we can bring him out here to have a look around. Perhaps we might come and visit you also."

"I'd love you to do that," Charlotte said. "My brother is coming to help me renovate the cabins. They're not ready yet, but please come and visit any time."

The chatter continued around the table and she finally felt comfortable and at ease.

"Do you like living at Forrest Glen?" Chelsea asked. "It is so different than the Gold Coast. No doubt you're missing the beaches and ocean."

"I haven't missed anything, especially not the crowds and traffic. Every day I wake up here I feel like it's a new adventure, a fresh start in life. A much slower pace." Charlotte looked around, the sky starting to have a hazy appearance as the winter afternoon waned. A jazz quartet played on the verandah of the house and music filled the area, the excited chatter of the guests a festive background noise. "I really do love where I live, and also the town. Everyone has been so friendly."

Ryan stood up to pour her another glass of champagne. "I originally came from further out west and this to me is the best land in the country. My brother here, comes and visits when he can."

Joe smiled at her. "When I'm not shearing, you'll find me here. Good place and good people."

Jaclyn sat up straighter and looked over towards another table set towards the back of the party area. "That looks like Alex's sister, Bridie, over there. And there's old Barney. Goodness me, I hardly recognised him dressed up. Such a lovely man."

Charlotte looked over towards the table. Picking up her drink she stood up. "Will you excuse me for a moment. I really must go and say hello to Barney and the others. I haven't seen him since we arrived together. I don't want him to think I've forgotten him. I'll come back soon."

Hunter stood up and pulled her chair back for her. "You do that, love. The others from town might be here then."

"Tell him we'll be over soon to see him," Marsha added.

"I will," she replied.

———

BARNEY WAVED as she approached and she tried to avert her eyes from Lester, who nodded slightly at her as she sat down next to Bridie, his crooked forced smile setting her nerves on edge. He'd dressed up for the occasion; a collared shirt and pressed trousers hung loose on his gaunt body. A full beard covered his weathered face, and a dangling silver cross hung from his ear. She drew her eyes away from him. Why did she always feel like he was staring at her, almost as if he was looking for something?

Bridie offered her some food and Charlotte turned

to her, complimenting her dress and shoes. She was an attractive woman, and Charlotte wondered not for the first time, why the hell she was with someone like Lester.

Thank goodness for Barney's interesting conversation, his knowledge of the horses and polo business holding her attention. When Marsha and Chen came over to say hello, she noticed Lester sat silently, not adding to the conversation. A couple of times she glanced across and caught him looking at her, always that leering smile when her eyes met his. Looking away quickly, an uneasiness filled her. He was fidgety, he never seemed to sit still and constantly played with the leather band he wore around his wrist. When Eli asked her to come with him to show some of the guests the stables and equine swimming pool, she took the opportunity, picking up her glass and following him to where a group stood waiting for the grand tour.

The group was mostly men, with only a couple of women. They all seemed to know each other and one of the men introduced everyone to her. "And your name is?" he asked.

Eli butted in. "This is Charlotte and she's my favourite person in the world."

She smiled. "Thank you, Eli."

"What an introduction," the man said.

"Which soapie are you in?" one of the women asked "I don't watch those shows so I'm not sure which one you beautiful young girls star in."

Charlotte laughed loudly, an amused look on her face as all eyes turned to her. "I'm not in any soapies. Are you kidding? I'm a primary school teacher who has taken a break from the life of education. I've bought the property next door." She pointed towards her house, the tin roof shining in the afternoon sun. "That beautiful old house over there and twenty hectares which I plan to turn into a writing and artist retreat is where I live."

One of the men took her arm. "Lead the way, Master Eli. Let's see what your old man has done to the place since the last time I visited."

The man who had taken her arm introduced himself as Edward. He was tall and thin, his arms toned and wiry. "Edward Visage. Pleased to meet you," he said, his dreamy blue eyes fixed on hers.

"Oh," she stammered. "Are you, *the* Edward Visage. The famous one."

One of the women came up beside them. "Don't let him bore you with his past feats."

"Please Mary, it's not always that someone recalls who I am, or rather who I was."

"I remember you well. "You're a famous equestrian rider. I watched you on TV when you won gold at the Olympics. Wow, wait until I tell my father. He loved watching you ride."

A look of delight covered his face and he bowed. "See, Mary. There are plenty who remember me."

One of the other men laughed. "Watch him, Charlotte. He's also on the lookout for someone to take to the Equestrian Ball next month. I hope you're not single."

Edward turned to her. "Now there's a question. Are you single?"

She ignored Eli who pulled at her arm. "I am. Yes, I'm single."

Edward linked her arm through his. "Well, maybe today was meant to be. Maybe there was a reason I drove all this way, rather than just to say happy birthday to my old mate."

▭

EDWARD LEANED over the table where the group had been sitting. He picked out a bottle of French champagne chilling in a silver bucket filled with ice. An amused expression crossed his face as he filled her glass. "Strange, Alex never told me he had such a beautiful neighbour. He's been keeping you a secret. I must have a chat with him about that."

She ignored his compliment, although it was flattering to have someone pay her such direct flirtatious attention. "I've only just moved in."

Edward raised one of his eyebrows. "I talk to Alex regularly. He usually lets me know if he has a single friend."

One of the women leaned over. "Perhaps he didn't want you to meet Charlotte. He knows you too well."

They all laughed and Charlotte took a long sip of her drink. The champagne tasted like the nectar of the gods and she took another mouthful. Edward was keen to know about her plans for the retreat and after she'd explained what she was aiming for she listened as he talked about his own life. He was forty, divorced, a retired professional equestrian and now liked to dabble in writing poetry and playing polo during the competition season. Alex and he had grown up together, ridden horses and motorbikes when they were teenagers, and divorced around the same time.

"I also have two children. They live with their mother so they're only with me sometimes. I might be interested in staying at one of your cabins once the place is up and running.' "

He was very attentive and suggested that perhaps he

might be interested in staying at one of the cabins once the place was up and running. When they returned from the tour he guided her back to his table.

Edward didn't leave her side. He was attentive, charming, and intelligent and she was intrigued by the business he ran. Like Alex, it was all about polo horses and events and she tried to follow his explanations of the different occasions that took place around the country and overseas.

Alex eventually made his way over to their group; Belinda was hanging tightly to his arm. They must have made up after their argument, she thought. She caught Alex's eye and they smiled at each other, both turning as Isla ran towards the group.

Isla made a beeline for her, pushing Edward's arm which was draped loosely on her shoulders out of the way. Climbing up onto Charlotte's lap, she snuggled in, only managing a nod when asked if she had eaten. She was worn out and unusually quiet. The excitement of the day proving to be too much and before long she was fast asleep.

Edward continued to talk and although Charlotte had been interested at the start, he had consumed too much alcohol and his conversation became solely about his business. He was becoming tedious but with Isla still on her lap it was difficult to get up and return to the table of locals. Her mind drifted off and she perused the different groups of guests dotted across the lawn. Barney had gone to sit in the stables. He'd told her he'd had enough of the socialising and he'd be there when she needed a lift home. Bridie had also left. Looking around, Charlotte located Lester, who stood in the shade of the sheds, a cigarette in his mouth as he observed the crowds of guests. She tried to look at him without him seeing her. The men on the other side of the table blocked Lester's view of her and she watched him as Edward's incessant voice droned in the background.

Lester drew back heavily on his cigarette, exhaling long straight reams of smoke. His eyes moved back and forth and if she didn't know better she would think he was casing each person out. Almost like a criminal does before he robs someone.

She froze, holding her breath as a memory came to her. She tried to think harder but Edward's voice broke the moment.

"Are you listening to me? I've just asked if you'd like to come to Sydney next weekend. I have a penthouse on the harbour. I'd love for you to come and stay. It's all on me." He put his hand on her arm, his fingers stroking her skin.

Before she could answer Alex's voice butted in. "I knew I shouldn't have left you alone with my good neighbour, Edward. No, Charlotte does not want to go to Sydney with you."

Edward hiccupped loudly before speaking. "Please let the lady answer for herself. There's nothing worse than a man telling a woman what she can and can't do."

Alex chuckled, although his face was serious. "Don't you be the pot calling the kettle black. You spent your entire life bossing women around."

Edward's voice was loud and slurred. "I think the beautiful lady can answer for herself."

Alex took a step toward Edward who had stood up. "I think you've had enough to drink."

Belinda came up behind Alex. "I'm sure Charlotte

can look after herself. Maybe a weekend away with Edward would do her good."

"See." Edward smirked. "The ladies know a good catch when they see one."

There was a cantankerous tone in Alex's voice. "I'd prefer it if you weren't trying to hit on my guests."

Edward hiccupped again and playfully put his fists up as if he wanted to fight Alex. "Ah, always the boring one. Thankfully I know how to give a gorgeous woman a good time."

Alex stepped forward but before he could answer, Charlotte spoke. Enough was enough. Her arms were aching from nursing Isla and her head was starting to pound from drinking alcohol in the sun. She made sure Edward could hear her clearly. "It's been lovely to meet you Edward and thank you for your kind invitation but I will have to say no."

"Maybe the weekend after," he suggested, placing his hand on her shoulder.

She stood up, passing Isla to Alex. Smiling sweetly, she removed Edward's hand, shook it and let it drop. "The answer is no. I'm not interested. Thank you once again."

Chapter 15

Lester watched the conversation between the group Charlotte was with. Fancy city mob, dressed up as if they were something special and acting like they were rich and famous. He hated all of them. These days you could look people up and seen how much wealth they had. Edward Visage was on the list of the richest people in Australia. Now look at him, he could hardly stand up properly and he was all over that stupid bitch who'd moved in next door.

His focus moved to Charlotte, watching her closely as she said goodbye to Alex and his brats. He'd had a better opportunity today to study her closely and he had listened with interest to her voice when she spoke. The very first time he'd got a decent look at her was when he'd driven Alex to get the kids from her place the other day. As soon as he'd seen her properly a stabbing jolt of panic had rippled through him. When she'd spoken, his gut had churned and he'd nearly forgotten to pat the bonnet of the car five times when he got out of it.

He knew her. He knew that face and voice.

Mustering his ability to show no emotion he'd kept his face expressionless, gritted his teeth, and acted like nothing was wrong. But it was there. A glint of reckoning, a memory packed away from years ago. There'd been an incident. He tried to read her thoughts, to see if there was a flash of recognition when she looked at him.

She might be good at hiding her thoughts, or perhaps she was so thick that she wouldn't remember him. He snarled inwardly. She wasn't that stupid. It was unlucky that she'd bought the property next door. Bridie should have worked harder on her brother and got him to purchase Forrest Glen. For all the talking and wheedling he'd done to try and get her to push him into it, Alex wouldn't come to the party. Stingy bastard. He had plenty of money. If Forrest Glen had been sold to Alex and put in his sister's name as Lester had suggested, he might have stuck around. Well, just for a while anyway. It would have given him more opportunity to get some more money behind him and have continual access to the hideout. He didn't want to own the property, it was just he didn't want anyone else to. It might stuff up his plans. At least with the old couple there had been no risk of anyone walking that far. Now with her next door, who knew how far she'd go. The other day he'd even felt as if someone was following him.

Even though he walked along exactly the same track and tied the gate in the same knots so as not to bring bad luck with different knots, he had the feeling that someone knew what he was up to. He'd carried a heavy stick with him. Just in case. There was no way he'd let anyone, no matter who it was, muck up his plans.

Maybe it had been Bridie. She had started to stand

up to him lately. The novelty had worn off and he knew it was only a matter of time before she'd buck up and tell him to leave. She might have been vulnerable when he first met her, but lately she'd started to answer him back and question some of his decisions. Women. He hated all of them.

He took a deep breath, a heaving loathing filling him as he watched the groups begin to leave. Be patient he chided himself. Don't draw attention to yourself. You're getting out of here soon. There would be plenty of opportunities to build on his wealth using idiots like the ones here today. He just needed to be patient and make sure that bitch next door didn't spoil anything.

Chapter 16

Barney dropped Charlotte home, the two of them chatting as the car chugged over the dirt road. Although Barney had sat quietly at the party she knew he didn't miss a beat. His eyes would have taken in everything. "What do you think about them all? Those guests there today?" Barney asked her.

She looked out the window at the horses poking their heads over fences, trying to find longer pickings on the other side. At times the paddocks could be fluoro-green, the pastures thick and plentiful. At other times the entire area could be thrust into drought, the earth bare and the ground turning to dust. She turned towards him.

"They're a different mob. I didn't even talk to any of Belinda's friends. She made me meet them all and I stood with them for a while but they just talked amongst themselves. I don't have the same interests that they do."

She didn't say any more. Everyone was different and they were probably all very nice people. It's just they were different to her, their career aims and what was important in life moving in a different direction to hers.

"And what do you think about the polo crowd?"

"Some of them were very interesting. I like hearing about their properties and where they live. I talked to an older couple who run a large establishment up in Queensland, they've even had Elton John perform a concert on their property." She sighed. "It really is the life of the rich and famous."

"And Edward?"

"Oh, Barney. You don't miss much do you?"

He looked at her, a twinkle in his eye. "I wondered how long it would take before he spotted you."

"I'm not silly. I mixed with plenty of people like that in my past life. Money means nothing to me and although Edward is probably a lovely man, he's not my type. Plus, I'm not looking for anyone. I'm well able to look after myself."

"Alex fired up a bit. I've not seen him like that with Edward before. He usually laughs him off."

She didn't reply, her mind whirling as she churned over the events of the day. "I noticed Eli and Isla got bored pretty quickly."

Barney turned into her driveway. "Yeah, they're a bit like me. It's not my crowd either but we did well to make an appearance for Alex. Sometimes I feel like he's on the outer with all that lot. He always seems to still be looking for something. At least now he's closer to the kids. He has you to thank for that."

She opened the car door. "Thanks, Barney. You're a good friend." She went to shut the door and then remembered something. "Barney, just something I was thinking about today, and please don't mention it to anyone, particularly Lester. I keep thinking I know him from somewhere. Do you know anything much about him before he came here?"

"I don't. He just appeared out of nowhere and no one seems to know anything about him. He told me once he was from Queensland but that's all he's ever said. All I know is that he's bad news. I saw him kick Jasper yesterday and I had a go at him about it. He threatened me, told me to watch out, I was old and easy to get rid of. Who says that sort of stuff? Bridie needs to give him the flick."

"Did you tell Alex?"

"I did. He said he's going to do something about him living here. The children only come for holidays but he said he doesn't want Lester anywhere near them."

"You wonder why Bridie is with him. She seems nice."

"She is. The trouble is she was married to a mongrel who never paid her any attention. Lester came along and put on a good show. She was lonely and she fell for it."

Charlotte pulled a face. "He gives me the creeps to tell you the truth."

"Yep, I get the same feeling. I think Bridie is starting to get sick of him also. She's said a few things to me lately and I wouldn't be surprised if she throws him out. The trouble is he might not go that easily."

"Let's hope he leaves soon." She waved goodbye and thanked him for the lift home.

THAT NIGHT for the first time since she'd arrived at Bindarra Creek Charlotte double-checked she'd locked her doors and windows. It never usually worried her being by herself and she wasn't sure why she was concerned tonight. In the distance she could hear the music still playing next door and she wondered if Edward had hooked up with one of Belinda's friends. They had been flocking around him by the time she'd found Barney to drive her home and then found Alex to say goodbye.

Alex had apologised. "I'm sorry I answered for you, but Edward is well known for the way he treats women. I hope you didn't mind."

"No, not at all, thank you. You saved me repeating my answer." His gaze had lingered on her face and she thought he had wanted to say more. His eyes were downcast and she wanted to wrap her arms around him and hug him tight. But that would be entirely inappropriate. She looked hard at him, her voice quiet. "Good night Alex and happy birthday."

———

AS SHE LAY in bed Charlotte went over the past few hours. She couldn't stop thinking about Alex and how he'd floated from one group to the other. He'd spent a lot of time talking to Barney down at the stables, another couple of men also standing with them, talking horses and polo. He had been obliging when Belinda got him to open his presents and cut his cake although her demands for a speech were ignored and he had made a quick exit back to the stables when she tried to drag him up for a dance.

Just before she left Charlotte had talked to Jaclyn, Chelsea and Marsha. Together they walked through the stables, stopping at the stalls to look at the horses that were settled for the night. A deep voice from behind them had sent a pleasant shiver through her body. "You really must bring your son, Gavin, over one day." Alex said, causing all of them to turn around.

"Oh, we will, thank you Alex," Marsha replied. "Actually, we're just about to leave. I have to pick him up. Thank you, it has been a very special night."

The women said their goodbyes. Two of them had babies they needed to get home to. "We would love to have stayed longer and I know I'll have to drag Hunter away, but I promised the baby-sitter we wouldn't be too late," Chelsea said.

As they said their goodbyes and gave Charlotte warm hugs, she thought how friendly everyone in town had been. The small community was what she needed. Bindarra Creek was her home. And that felt good.

As the women walked ahead, her head spun. Too much champagne and also now it was just her and Alex. His eyes settled on her and she looked down. "It's really time I went home."

"Barney will drive you. I apologise for Edward."

Her gaze met his. "I'm able to look after myself, don't worry.'

They stood and stared at each other. The air was still in the stables and the lights dim. Moths clustered around the globes, their tapping noises and the shuffling of one of the horses the only sound inside. Outside the music played and occasionally a loud laugh or yell could be heard. Neither spoke and Alex's look made her want to reach up and stroke his face. His eyes were sad, not how he should look on his birthday.

Together they'd walked back out, thankfully not too

far behind the ladies, because as soon as Alex appeared, Belinda had raced over and grabbed him, her voice shrill and uneven. "Come with me. It's photo time." His shoulders had slumped and he had not looked back as Belinda dragged him over towards the house where a photographer was set up taking group photos. Belinda however had taken a sneaky look over her shoulder at Charlotte. Almost a look of… he's mine!

BELINDA'S GROUP was probably still partying. They had all been making the most of the alcohol and Charlotte had seen quite a few of them—Belinda included—popping brightly coloured pills in the bathroom.

Charlotte pulled the covers up higher as the old house creaked, the chill of the winter night air replacing the warmth of the day. A possum jumped onto the roof, the loud bang it made when it landed startling her. She got up and turned a light on. Usually, she slept in complete darkness but tonight for some reason she needed some light. As she lay listening to the noises outside she lectured herself not to imagine things. Those noises, however, did sound exactly like someone walking on the verandah. Lying still, she held her breath, a scraping sound, very much as if a chair had been pushed across the verandah floorboards, sending a chill through her body.

Perhaps the possum was out there, looking for fruit or crumbs from morning tea. Reaching over she turned her bedside lamp on, listening carefully. The stairs creaked and her eyes darted around the room. She reached for her phone. If someone tried to break in through the windows or doors she'd have to ring the police. Barney didn't have a mobile phone and Alex would still be partying.

She sat up, listening carefully for a long while. Her windows were frosted glass and through them she could see the shadows of the tree branches outside, brushing back and forth. The moonlight reflected on the panes of glass, its luminance throwing shafts of light across her room. If she got up and opened the window she would see if there was anyone out there. She hesitated. Perhaps that wasn't the safest thing to do.

There were no further noises on the verandah, only the sound of the possum thumping across the roof. Her eyes lifted to the ceiling and she envisaged where it was, its screeching calls loud in the quietness of the night as it jumped from the roof to the tree next to her room. There must have been two of them, she thought. One on the verandah and one on the roof. She lay back down, the bedside lamp still on, her phone tight in her hand. It would be good to have Jacob in the house at night and she hoped it wasn't too long until he visited. The tree branches rustled and soon the possum was quiet. Eventually, sleep came to her, the house silenced as the clouds passed over the moon, cloaking the area in darkness.

When she woke early in the morning her light was still on and she reached over to flick it off. Her eyes were heavy and she lay back down, closing them and going over the people she'd met at the party. She remembered the noises she had heard last night. Everything always seemed so much worse at night and now as flickers of sunlight filtered in she was annoyed that she'd been scared and imagined someone had been on the verandah.

She thought about the party, Belinda, Edward and Alex. Alex was unhappy. Perhaps it was just a bad stage in the relationship and he'd get through it and work it out. He was probably in a slump. No doubt they'd probably worked it out last night. Both he and Belinda had nothing to complain about, after all, there was plenty of money, a thriving business that he was passionate about, and good friends.

And two beautiful children.

Closing her eyes, she dozed a little, remembering the famous faces that had been in attendance and the friendly table of local people. She thought about Isla and how cute she had looked, dressed up. Eli had seemed so grown up, showing everyone around and telling them about the property. Formal attire had made Barney look like a different person and it had been good of him to drive her home. And then there was Lester. The sight of him standing near the shed smoking his cigarette came into her mind, the way his eyes glinted and narrowed when he talked to her.

She sat upright, her eyes wide open, her heart pounding hard. She remembered. It came to her in a flash who he reminded her of. Did he just look like him or was it him? It was over fifteen years ago. People changed a lot in that time, or if you wanted to change or become not so recognisable it could be easily done.

You could grow a beard, lose weight and wear glasses. A shaved head instead of hair and even new teeth where once there were noticeable gaps. A changed name, a respectable partner, and a new area to live in where no one knew you, or would think to look.

Charlotte's stomach churned, an uneasy anxiousness pressing down as she relived the memory. Many years ago, just before she turned twenty, she had worked in a bank. There had only been a year to go of her education studies but instead of completing the final twelve months, she'd wanted a change. Taking time off from her course she got a job in a bank. The break from study was what she needed and after a couple of years, she felt invigorated and returned to complete her course. Once she graduated she taught in a couple of country towns before meeting Hugh at the races at Dalby. She'd fallen head over heels in love. Her first real relationship and she'd had no qualms following him back to the Gold Coast, marrying, and trying to fit into his way of life. At the time she thought it was what she wanted; marriage, a house, and kids. Pregnancy hadn't happened. Perhaps that was a blessing. At least when it ended, it was a clean break and she never needed to see him again.

Now, her mind reeled back to the bank days. She'd worked at a small branch on the south side of Brisbane. It was in a quiet position and only busy early in the morning and just before closing time. Situated in a group of a few shops, most customers were local pensioners, or workers from the businesses nearby. The staff knew most of the customers by name and the vibe was relaxed and casual.

One Friday when the manager and accountant went on their usual end of the week, long lunch to the nearby pub, Charlotte and four other staff were left to run the place. They weren't worried, the next hour was usually quiet and it wouldn't be until after two o'clock—just before they wanted to close their tills—that customers would roll in.

Her co-workers, Leila and Sarah were all around the same age, and Peter—who was supposed to be in charge while the others were at lunch— was only a few years older. They were a fun group of people to work with and similar to her, all single. That meant Friday nights and weekends were spent drinking and dancing, partying the nights away until the early hours of the morning. They'd recover on weekends by sunbaking on the golden beaches of the Sunshine Coast, swimming and relaxing, getting ready for the next big night out. It was a perfect life, carefree, fun, and full of social events.

They'd all been out the back of the teller's boxes discussing plans for the weekend. The city was lively on a Friday night and they'd head in there for early drinks and then dinner, with dancing and more drinking to come afterward. Taxis there and back were cheap and Peter lived close to town, providing a perfect place to crash after a big night.

The girls were discussing what they'd wear when a man wearing dark clothes and a beanie leapt over the counter, positioning himself directly in front of them. Charlotte stared directly into the barrel of a sawn-off shotgun, pointed straight at the four of them. The man yelled not to move and to do as he said. Her heart had been like a hammer in her chest as he waved the gun wildly in the air. Much of what happened next was a blur, the bruises left on Peter's arm from where she gripped it, testament to how frightened she was.

At one point the gun was pushed up against Leila's back and the man motioned for her to gather the money in the bag he passed her. His voice was angry, but shaky, when he spoke. "No one move! Stand where you are! Otherwise, I'll shoot the lot of you."

At the same time, a middle-aged man who was a regular customer, entered through the bank doors. The robber turned the gun on him, yelling at him to lie down on the floor and keep his hands above his head. The customer flattened himself on the floor and she could still remember how red his bald head was as he lay there, helpless to provide any assistance.

Leila had emptied the money out of the teller boxes, even adding to it from the cases kept below the shelf. The regimented staff training kicked in and no one cared what went in the bag. The instructions were to give robbers whatever they wanted. Bank money was insured and in the past there had been shootings and even deaths from staff making stupid decisions and not handing over whatever was asked for.

Charlotte had no intention of being a hero and from the look on the others' faces, neither did they. Her head had pounded.

Just take the money and go. Give it to him quickly and get him out of here. Soon there would be mothers coming in with little kids, going to the bank before they picked the older kids up from school. Her body had shaken and she felt like she wanted to throw up.

Leila was ordered to return to the others. The man kept waving the gun around and Charlotte's eyes had followed its movements. She'd never been close to a gun before or even seen a real one. The only ones she'd seen were the ones on TV, in those movies where the bank robbers took everyone hostage and then killed some of them off before they made their getaway.

She'd been transfixed by the robber and his gun, the image of him and the scratched gun barrel cemented in her mind. The man was thickset and short, with long hair that hung like scraggy rats' tails on his shoulders. His eyes stared hard at them and she thought he looked like he was on drugs, his movements jerky and nervous. When he'd first burst in he'd worn a bandanna across his face, but as he became more and more animated he'd let it slip down and she'd been transfixed by the missing teeth in his mouth.

His face was thin, his eyes steely and when he turned towards her, his stare fixed on her and she thought she was going to pass out.

"Who can open the safe?" He waved his gun in her face. "You?"

She nodded. Only last week the manager had shown her the combinations and how to unlock the large safe. It was good training, he'd said.

The safe door was heavy and thick and set in the middle were two combination locks. The manager had allowed her to reset and use her own numbers, but now her mind scrambled to remember them.

Peter touched her on the arm. "It's okay, Charlotte. You can do it."

Combinations often didn't go right the first time and she took a deep breath as the end of the gun pushed into her back. "Hurry up. Open it," the robber had mumbled.

Standing in front of the safe, she spoke quietly, her words tumbling out. "You're making me nervous. Please take the gun from my back." She didn't turn around when she spoke, but she knew her words were heard when she felt the pressure release from her spine. Taking a deep breath, she tried to remember the numbers, spinning the combination wheels around, back and forth, two this way, seven the other, and three back again.

The robber came right up beside her. "What's the problem?"

At that moment she was sure they were all going to die. The man's eyes were cold and the silver earring hanging from his ear swayed like a slow pendulum on a time bomb, ticking slowly, about to explode. His breath was rank and she'd pulled back, her teeth clenched together as she focused once more on the locks.

"I'll do it again," she said, her words sounding loud in the silence. This time she blocked any distractions and concentrated hard. She'd always been good with numbers. She might not be able to remember people's names, but numbers were her thing. She could recite the number plates of cars from years ago and had memorised every bank branch number in the state. It was what she liked about the bank. Working with numbers, day in and day out. Now her life and the others next to her, as well as the poor man still lying face down in the public area, depended on her, and her recall of numbers.

She flicked the dials back and forth, counting and talking out loud as she went. Right then left, two then seven, pushing in hard, and yes. It clicked. She had it. Pulling hard on the handle she swung open the heavy door. The man pushed his gun toward all of them. "Get the money for me and then you all get in there."

The others grabbed whatever cash there was and filled the bags he held out. When he was sure they had handed everything over, he motioned with his gun to move to the back of the safe. Giving them a final sneer, he called out, "Adios," before slamming the door behind him as he exited. Charlotte heard the wheel spin as he left. They were locked in.

Peter had managed to find the phone positioned on

the wall of the safe as well as a safety torch. The three girls stood in shock, their faces white, shaking as they listened to Peter telling whoever was on the other end what had happened and where they were.

That afternoon had consisted of police interviews and filling in forms. The customer who was forced onto the floor sat with them, his hands still trembling as he tried to write down what he had witnessed. He was the local dentist and had come to the bank to sign a document. He felt helpless not being able to help them, but he agreed with Charlotte that it appeared the man was high on something, aggravated and jumpy.

They all gave explicit descriptions and Charlotte could describe the gun perfectly, down to the last little scratch on its timber part. In the dim light as the robber was shutting the door, she had also noticed a small tattoo on the back of his neck. For a moment his greasy hair had flicked sideways and between the strands, the tattoo had appeared for a split second. None of the others had noticed it and she wasn't a hundred percent sure of its shape. The police wrote the details down, noting that "possible small tattoo of an anchor - middle back of the neck."

On Monday they'd all been back at work, nervous from the robbery, but bolstered by a big weekend of drinking and re-telling the story. They considered themselves lucky that at least the gun hadn't been fired. A robbery two weeks earlier at another nearby branch had resulted in gunshots through the roof of the bank building and staff forced to lie on the floor with a gun held to their heads.

"Lucky." That's what her parents and Aunt Lucille told her and that maybe it was time to get out of the bank and back to what she always wanted to do; teach and work with children.

She hadn't thought about her bank days for a long time. She rolled on her side and tried to recall the day of the holdup. Lester was short, wiry and his face thin. The other man had been a bit stockier but his face was similar. She wished she had a photo of the bank robber, but he'd never been caught. The police said he'd done other holdups and they were chasing him for several crimes. Sometimes he worked alone but other times he had a partner, another man who had been with him when they'd held up an armoured guard truck about to drop off a large amount of money to one of the banks. That one had gone wrong and ended up with one of the guards being shot. He hadn't died but his injuries were serious.

Years later, Peter contacted her and let her know they'd caught the other man. Not the one who had held them up, but his accomplice on the other jobs. Mysteriously the accomplice died not long after he went to jail. An inmate, who was apparently paid off, fatally stabbed him. Peter had still been working in the bank when he'd rung her to let her know the latest police information. Now he was high up in the loans section, nowhere near money or tellers with risk of hold-ups. A police contact he'd kept over the years had passed the latest information onto him. "They've never caught the fella who did us though," he said to Charlotte. "I wonder where he is, or if he's still alive?"

Chapter 17

The next three days gave Charlotte a chance to mull over the memories and connections she had recalled. She hadn't seen Isla and Eli, and she suspected everyone was busy cleaning up, entertaining guests who had stayed, and getting over the late night. She wanted to talk to Alex. Perhaps she was imagining what she suspected. What was it about Lester that reminded her of the robber? Was it just because he wore a similar earring? Because apart from that and a bad feeling about him she had nothing else to go on. She also needed to let Alex and Barney know she was going up to Jacob's place for a couple of days. He was struggling after the breakup with his girlfriend and it would be a chance to catch up with her parents. She also needed to remove herself from Alex's company for a while. Thoughts of him continually filled her mind and she needed to get away and sort herself out.

She wandered slowly across the paddocks, enjoying watching the horses in Alex's yards as they stood gazing back at her. A couple of them bucked and cavorted, galloping in the other direction, their hooves pounding over the grassy slopes before standing at a distance. They swung their heads, rearing playfully as they watched her.

A small storm had passed over the previous night and it was just enough to freshen the paddocks. There was supposed to be more rain coming and she knew that would please the locals and farmers who waited for the wet days to arrive. Most of the area was used for crops and livestock, and when the farmers prospered, everyone did, the effect filtering through to the township and the people who worked in it.

She didn't see Alex until she was near to the house. The sun had been in her eyes, however she knew from where he sat he must have been able to see her as she walked towards him. Jasper was asleep at his feet, his long nose resting on Alex's boots. When Alex stood up to greet her, the dog yawned before settling back down to his slumber.

Alex was sitting on the verandah by himself, a cup of coffee in his hand. He gave her a quick smile before pulling a chair out for her to sit on. "The kids are inside. I put a movie on for them. They're still worn out from helping me clean up over the last few days."

She bent down and stroked Jasper, wondering where Belinda was. "It was a lovely night."

His gaze settled directly on hers. "I wanted to thank you for the painting. It really is special." He took a sip of his coffee. "It means a lot to me."

"It's just something small. I had no idea what to get you."

"It's perfect. Can I offer you a coffee?" He stood up

and walked towards the kitchen. "Sit here and I'll get you one."

She sat looking out over the smaller yards near the house. The horses were content and fat, and a mare stood patiently, a leggy foal pushing and shoving at her as it fed.

Alex soon appeared with her coffee. "I had to sneak in and get it. I don't want the kids to know you're here."

"Thank you. It's just what I feel like," she said.

"I want to tell you something." He sat down and her stomach twisted, her heart thumping hard as he looked at her. She had developed feelings for him and she'd need to stop whatever it was she was thinking. It wasn't fair. He wasn't single.

"Why do you look at me like that sometimes?' he asked. "It's almost as if you want to say something, but then you don't." A smile touched his mouth and she sipped her coffee, staring at his lips. She turned her eyes away from him. Was she that easy to read?

She managed to keep her voice even. "What was it you wanted to tell me because I also came to tell you something?"

He stretched his legs out in front of him, crossing them at the ankles. She noticed he was in old clothes again; shorts with ragged edges and a T-shirt that was so faded she couldn't read what was on the front.

"Ladies first," he murmured. "Tell me what you came over to say."

"I'm going away for a few days. To Tamborine Mountain, and then Brisbane to see my parents. Jacob is at home on the mountain and he's struggling a bit after his break-up. I thought if I went now then I'd be back ready, in time to get the cabins more organised for my first guests."

He hesitated, before nodding. "Sounds like a plan. I thought your brother was going to come and stay with you for a while."

"He was, but not everything is going to plan for him. Besides, I'm going to be here for a long time. He can come when he's ready. His life hasn't quite gone as he thought it would. I think he needs a bit of support."

Alex put his cup down. "Sounds familiar, life not going as planned. That's what I wanted to talk to you about." He watched the mare and foal, his words steady and even. "I've broken up with Belinda. She's left. Gone back to Sydney."

Charlotte sat upright, plonking her cup down so hard it nearly broke. "Jees, what happened? She was telling me all about the wedding plans the other night."

"Look I don't want to get into it too much. It's still a bit raw and I feel like a mongrel because it's me who broke it off. I told you weeks ago. I wasn't happy. I'm not sure how it got this far but I can't let it go any further. It isn't fair to either her or me. I don't love her."

"I'm so sorry, Alex. No wonder you look so worried." She went to ask how the kids felt about it but thought better. It was as if he read her mind.

"Of course, the kids are happy. It suits them perfectly." He managed a smile. "When are you leaving?"

Her mind whirled with what he'd just told her. Thank goodness she was going away. That would give her time to reassess her feelings. "I'll go tomorrow and be back by Friday. I thought I'd let you know so the kids don't come and visit and also to ask if you could keep an eye on the place." She didn't want to admit that she'd been paranoid the other night and imagined someone walking along the verandah. Now was also not the time to explain that her imagination was running wild and that in her head she thought that Lester looked very similar to a bank robber from fifteen years ago. There were possibly hundreds of men that age who looked just like that and it was so long ago. It was too much of a coincidence.

Chapter 18

Time away visiting Jacob did Charlotte the world of good. Her brother was sliding into a hole of hatred and depression. She remembered the feeling. His house was a mess and his attitude to everything was negative. She took over the minute she arrived. It was good to feel needed and doing the washing, sorting out the household, and stocking his pantry was energising. "There is nothing in the fridge except alcohol and cheese," she said, screwing up her face at the sight of mouldy vegies and fruit rotting in the crisper.

"Thanks Charlie. I don't know what I'd do without you."

Now, even after a day, there was a difference. Jacob looked more like himself after a shower, a shave and some help from her sorting out his clothes. Together they went through anything that didn't belong to him, taking great joy in filling up the rubbish bin with anything that reminded him of Cecilia.

Charlotte had taken him out to dinner at the local Indian restaurant and they laughed about childhood times, reminding each other that they'd always have each other, no matter what happened.

"So, when are you coming down to help me out," she asked, the two of them now back home after eating way too much at the restaurant. They sat on his front verandah. "There is always room for a glass of red to wash all that food down," Jacob said, burping loudly as she laughed with him. "God, Cecilia used to have a fit when I burped like that. Not that I ever did it in public. When she left she told me I was uncouth, boring and had no motivation to better myself."

"You're better off without her, just like I am without Hugh. Cecilia could never stand that you didn't continually fuss over her or that you didn't want to climb the ladder at work. Just because she wanted all of that or needed to look a million dollars from the minute she got out of bed in the morning until she went to sleep doesn't mean that we all had to be like that." She leaned in against him, giving him a gentle shove with her shoulder. "You and I are very alike. Thanks goodness we've now worked out what's important in life. I guess Mum and Dad taught us that."

Jacob took a large sip of his wine. "Yes, them and Aunt Lucille."

"I miss her so much," Charlotte twirled the glass in her hand. "There's rarely a day goes past that I don't think of her."

"She'd be happy with what you've done with her money. Family meant so much to her."

"She would be happy. It's a shame there are no kids between us though. Poor Mum and Dad. No hope of grandkids."

"Don't say that, Charlotte. You'll meet someone one

day. You've still got some time up your sleeve. Your biological clock is ticking though."

"I know. You don't need to remind me."

Jacob was only two years older than she was. He raised an eyebrow. "At least I can always find someone younger. Men have more time up their sleeve."

"Everything is easier for men, isn't it?"

"Now, don't get jaded. We aren't all the same." He filled her glass up. "You seem to talk a lot about those kids and, what's his name, next door to you. What's the go there?"

She shrugged. "Alex is lovely. He just broke off his engagement. I think he's a bit mixed up. We're good friends and I do love those kids." She looked out into the darkness, an owl staring straight back at her from a nearby tree. "I think that owl is listening to us."

"Don't try and side-track me. Keep going. What about this fella next door? I know you too well. I reckon you're keen on him."

"I don't want another man. Alex is a friend, that's all."

Jacob chuckled. "You make me laugh, Charlie, and I can read you like a book. It's so good to see you. Perhaps a visit to Bindarra Creek is what I need."

She sat up straight. "It would be awesome if you came down. There is also something I wanted to talk to you about. It goes back to the time I got held up in the bank. Do you remember that?"

"Of course, I do. It's a while ago though. What's happened to make you want to talk about it?"

CHARLOTTE DID a lot of thinking on the drive back down to Bindarra Creek. She took the inland route, stopping at the small towns for coffee and browsing through the art galleries and antique shops. There had been decent rainfall in the region and the hills and paddocks were covered in lush grass, the cows were fat, and the small creeks she crossed running rapidly. Excitement filled her as she neared home and she waved to a few of the locals as she drove through the township.

When she stopped to get bread from the bakery, she ran into Jaclyn Rossiter.

"It was good to see you at Alex's party," Jaclyn said. "But we didn't get to talk much. That good looking fellow had a grip on you."

Charlotte laughed. "Don't worry, I gave him the flick. Way out of my league," she said with a smile.

Jaclyn had been the principal at the local school but was on maternity leave. 'You know I'm loving the break from school life," Jaclyn said. 'Any chance of you coming in to work? I know the school's always chasing good teachers."

"Not at the moment," Charlotte replied. "I'm also enjoying a change."

They'd chatted for a while and Charlotte had admired Jaclyn's baby who was tucked up asleep in the pram. When they parted ways, Jaclyn gave her a friendly hug and promised to catch up for a coffee in the next few weeks.

It wasn't often that Charlotte went into town but when she did the people were friendly and they all seemed to know who she was and what she had planned for Forrest Glen. It was a typical country town where everyone knew each other and what was going on.

As she started the car she thought back to conversations she'd had with Jacob. His questions had forced her to think honestly about her feelings for Alex. Every time she saw him made her realise that her feelings had changed. Now she was attracted to him in a different way However just because he'd split with Belinda didn't make it right to reveal how she felt. It was only right that she avoided seeing him so often and give him time to work out his relationship. It was highly likely that they'd get back together. It was important to tread carefully.

There was also the problem of Lester. Jacob hadn't been much help with that topic. He reminded her that years ago she had a similar flashback. This wasn't the first time she thought she'd seen the guy who'd robbed the bank.

After the holdup she'd transferred to a different branch where she'd worked as a teller for a short while. One morning she had been serving customers when she looked up to greet the next person in line. The man who stood in front of her looked the same as the robber. Trying to remain calm and not draw attention to herself she served him just like any other customer. All she wanted was to give him the hundred dollars that he was withdrawing and get him out of the building. However, something went wrong with the transaction and there hadn't been enough money in his account to complete his request. She'd mumbled and tried to make an excuse. By the time she'd called the manager over to assist, the man had grabbed his bank book and left.

She hadn't been confident enough to report it. He looked like the robber but with short hair and a thicker build. It was only a few weeks after that she left the bank for good, putting the holdup and the image of the bank robber behind her. Connections like that made her nervous. What if he recognised her?

Were the two sightings, one not long after the holdup and now one fifteen years later, coincidences of someone who looked similar? Was her mind playing tricks on her? She hoped so. Hopefully, Lester might move on. Alex had confided in Charlotte before she left for Jacob's that he was trying to convince Bridie to kick him out, to get rid of him. Maybe Lester would be gone when she returned. She could only hope so.

Chapter 19

Charlotte was nearly home when the light started to fade, the sun dipping behind the western hills. Lights from Alex's house flickered through the trees as she followed the road that led to her property and she wondered how he was going and what the kids had been up to in the three days she'd been away. Thoughts of him crept into her mind and she tried hard to push them away. Something in their relationship had shifted and it niggled and confused her. The visit to Jacob's place had put her life into perspective once again, and now she wanted to get back and focus on the business.

As soon as she unlocked the front door, she knew something was amiss. Flicking the light on she stared in dismay. The contents of her cupboards and sideboard were strewn across the floor, books taken out of her bookcase also joining the mess on the floor. She inhaled sharply and slowly backed out. Whoever had been in there might well still be there. Bolting back to the car she started the engine and flew out through the gates and down the driveway. She slowed down once she was out of sight of the house and pushed Alex's number on her phone.

Eli answered it and she tried to keep her voice calm. "Hi, Eli. Yes, I had a nice holiday. Could you please put your dad on? It's important to get him quickly."

Alex had been down at the stables and by the time she talked to him, she was near to his place. She was shaken, her voice fraught. "I've been broken into. I've only opened the front door and seen all my stuff over the floor. I'm in the car now, not far from your place. I'm worried they're still in the house."

There was an urgency in Alex's reply. "I'm down at the stables. Drive in there." She could hear him telling Eli to run and get Isla.

As she pulled in beside the stables she spotted Alex, standing next to the entrance to the building. Eli and Isla ran from the house and the three of them jumped in her car. "I've probably panicked," she said, the sight of Alex calming her instantly. Thank goodness she had him to depend on. "I was just worried whoever broke in is still there. I probably should have rung the police straight away."

"Don't be silly. It was the best decision to ring me first. At least you're safe. Let's have a quick look and then we can ring the police."

ALEX MADE the three of them stay in the car while he checked the perimeter of the house before peering in through the front doorway.

"There's no one in there. It looks like they've broken in through the back door. I can see where the door has been levered open. You kids stay on the verandah.

Charlie and I will just have a quick look and then ring the police. No one touch anything."

Everything Charlotte owned was scattered across the floor. Drawers and cupboards were open and the surfaces of tables and cupboards cleared, the contents strewn widely. Cards, papers, and mementos were tipped out, every box emptied and cushions taken off lounge chairs.

"They were looking for something, or anything of value I guess," she said.

Alex shook his head, holding Isla's hand and telling Eli not to touch anything. "We were home during the day, and only out one night while you were away. There hasn't been anyone around."

"Whoever it was isn't very smart." A cushion lay on the floor and she picked it up and placed it back on the lounge. "I can see they've taken some alcohol I had in the rack there and there's a box gone from here that I had all my cards in." She took a deep breath. "The really valuable items are those paintings still hanging on the wall."

Alex placed his hand on her shoulder, the warmth of his touch, soothing yet also sending fluttering sensations through her body. She pulled herself together as he continued to ply her with questions. "Do you have jewellery they might have taken? That's usually the other thing they go for."

She held out her hands, the gold antique ring with a blue square stone in it fixed firmly on her finger. "This is my most treasured item. It was Aunt Lucille's and I rarely take it off. I have other jewellery but it's not really valuable."

They made their way through the mess on the floor

toward her bedroom. She gasped when she saw how every drawer had been tipped out, her underwear and nighties spread across the bed, other bits of clothing tipped in piles on the floor.

A jewellery box that had taken pride of place in the centre of her dressing table was missing. Her father had made it for her when she was a teenager and it had been full of her costume jewellery and silver bracelets. "They weren't worth any money, just sentimental value." Tears welled in her eyes. "The box meant a lot to me though."

Isla gripped her hand and squeezed, looking up at Charlotte, a concerned look on her little face. Charlotte made sure her voice was calm.

"It's okay Isla, don't look so worried."

Alex wrapped his arm around Charlotte's shoulders. "C'mon and we'll ring the police. They'll want to finger-print the place. This hardly ever happens, although there have been a couple this year which the locals say is very uncommon."

The police arrived shortly after Alex called them. Constables Donaldson and Morgan offered their sympathy. "So sorry, Charlotte, that someone would do this to you," Morgan said. "Break-ins are rare around here and it's more than likely someone from out of town who did it. People drive out here from the coast, looking for remote houses. They would have been after money and jewellery by the looks of it."

"I'm so happy they didn't take your records or record player," Eli said.

"Or the drawings Eli did for you," Isla added in. "I'm sad that they took the box your dad made for you."

She hugged them both. "They didn't have much to take really. I'd say they were a bit disappointed."

Constable Donaldson took her details. "We'll be back in the morning to take photos and go over the place for fingerprints or anything else that might give some clues. Do you have somewhere to stay the night? You can't stay in here while it's like this? You might …"

Alex interrupted the conversation. "Charlotte can stay at our place. There are plenty of spare rooms."

All of a sudden, she was tired. Her eyes roved around the room. The long drive and then arriving home to this pressed down on her and all she wanted to do was have something to eat and put her head down on a comfortable pillow.

Isla clutched at her hand. "You're sleeping at our place. I can read a book to you and we can talk before you go to sleep. I have a special pillow you can have and…"

"Okay, Isla, less chatter now. Charlotte is tired," Alex pulled Isla back and hung onto her, stopping her from jumping up and down and pulling on Charlotte's arm.

She was too tired to argue and besides it made sense. "Thank you. That's kind of you and I will take you up on the offer. It won't be far to come in the morning and I can come over here early." She didn't add that she'd also feel safe at Alex's. The fact that someone had easily entered her house was unsettling and she imagined someone creeping around, finding their way in. What if she had been home? Had they known the house was empty?

She shivered as Alex's concerned face peered down at her. "The police want to know what time in the morning you'll be back here."

Her mind drifted off and she missed what they were

saying. "I just need to sleep." She muttered, following Isla to the car.

They waited for Alex who stood and talked to the police for a bit longer before walking around the house and making sure it was locked up.

"It doesn't matter anyway," she said as he hopped into the car. "There's nothing left to take. They were too stupid to realise the value of the paintings and rugs. I decided when I moved here to keep it basic."

Alex served her up a huge bowl of spaghetti Bolognese, leftovers from the night before. The four of them ate together and soon the kids had her laughing with their stories of what they'd been up to while she'd been away. Alex asked about her parents and when Jacob was coming to visit. She reminded him that she had guests arriving in the coming months. There was quite a bit to do before the cabins were ready and Jacob would arrive before then to help her set up properly.

A large glass of wine helped her relax even more and Alex ignored the time and let the kids sit up with them until after ten o'clock. In the end, Isla fell asleep on her lap, her long eyelashes dark against her cheeks, her soft breathing and warm body a comforting feeling after the long day.

There were a few spare rooms to choose from but Alex suggested the one next to Isla's. "She will love that you are right next door to her. No doubt she will be knocking on your door early in the morning. Don't let her come in too early. You look tired, make the most of a sleep in."

He'd made the bed up. "Clean sheets and we just bought this new mattress. You should sleep like a baby.

Don't get up early. The police aren't going to be there until nine."

She watched as he threw another blanket on the bed and flicked a bedside lamp on.

Relief filled her. It was a while since anyone had fussed over her and she drew her eyes away from watching him as he turned to her.

"Thank you," she said, "I'll sleep well."

"The bathroom is there with everything you need. This is set up as a guest room." Alex paused before opening the blinds. The light of the moon shone through the slats, the paddocks and stable visible beyond the window. "This bedroom has a lovely view. In the morning you can lie in and enjoy it. Night, Charlie."

The door closed behind him as he left and she flopped back on the bed. The room was fitted out with white and grey glossy furniture. It reminded her of the flash houses on the coast and she grimaced when she noticed the standard prints on the wall. The plush carpet was soft under her feet and when she opened the bathroom door she recoiled with dismay. Black glossy tiles on the floor were matched by grey and gold trimmings and feature tiles. She giggled. This had to be Belinda's decorating. She remembered her bragging about doing up the bathrooms. There were three sinks across the far wall, each with its own set of gold taps and faucets, a mirror taking up the entire wall behind them. Next to the basins was the shower, big enough for a party she thought.

The bathroom was as big as her bedroom and lounge put together. How the other half lived.

Sleep came easily and she would have slept for much longer, except at seven o'clock she awoke to someone standing beside her. Isla stood staring at her, her gorgeous green eyes looking into hers. "Dad said I could come in now. He said it was okay."

Charlotte rolled over and made room for the little girl who snuggled in beside her.

"Maybe don't talk for a few minutes, Isla. Just let me wake up."

They lay together, looking through the blinds. In the yard below, Alex was on a tractor, towing a trailer with feed for the horses. Eli sat on top of the bales, and Barney and Jasper walked slowly behind. It was feed time and they watched as the horses tossed their heads and nipped at each other, pushing to get to the feed first.

Soft light filtered across the paddocks, the green and gold of the grasses swaying in the early morning breeze. Charlotte leaned on one elbow. From here she could see her house, the yard fence, and even a glimpse of the cubbyhouse in the poinciana tree. Further beyond was the row of bushes that lined the creek, the hills behind the far gate outlined, distinct on such a clear day.

Isla sat up and stared through the window also. "The hills are pretty this morning. You can see them clearly. Sometimes there's too much dust or the clouds and fog go over them."

"I'm going to explore them one day," Charlotte said. "We could walk from my place and take a packed lunch. They say there are caves there."

"Barney said the bushrangers used to hide in them. That was in the olden days. Before there were cars."

"We'll plan a day there. We might have to get a map so we know where we're going."

Isla bounced up and down on the bed. "Can we go today?"

Thoughts of the break-in brought Charlotte back to reality with a reckoning thump. She flopped back on the pillow. "No, today I have grown-up chores to do."

They looked at each other and grinned, speaking at the same time. "Ain't nobody got time for that!"

Chapter 20

The police were thorough and sifted through the house, dusting for fingerprints wherever they could. They also inspected outside, searching for car tracks, however apart from where Charlotte had driven in last night, there were none.

"I'd say they parked near the gate," Constable Shultz said. "Maybe on the grass there. It was windy last night and the dust has probably blown over the markings."

"Unless they walked," Isla butted in.

Alex raised his eyebrows and looked toward Charlotte.

"How about we go and find some books for you to read." She took Isla's hand and headed towards where the bookcase had been emptied onto the floor. "The police have said they have done everything they need to here. You can help me, Isla. We'll put all these books back in where they're supposed to go. It's time to sort through everything and try and work out if there is anything else missing."

Charlotte hoped they'd talked the break-in down and not made too much fuss about someone gaining entry to her house. The last thing she wanted was for the children to be worried about it happening to them. Isla was subdued though as she turned the pages of her favourite book.

Charlotte pulled the little girl's hair back and braided it into one long plait that hung down to the middle of her back. In a month it would be time for the children to return to school and Alex had commented this morning that he wanted some time to talk to her about options for their education. She wondered if all the children's nagging and wheedling had prompted him to think about letting them go to the Bindarra Public School instead of boarding so far away. With Belinda out of the way, there was no reason for them not to stay with him.

Isla shut the book she was looking at and looked up at Charlotte. She pursed her lips and narrowed her eyes. "I think Lester did it."

Trying not to look shocked, Charlotte took her time replying, checking to see if Alex was nearby. He wasn't. He was outside talking to the police. Charlotte lowered her voice. "Did what?" she asked.

Isla stood up and put both hands on her hips. "I think he broke in here and took your jewellery and boxes."

"What makes you say that?"

Isla sounded like she was a detective and was obviously using her most grown-up voice. She folded her arms for an added dramatic effect. "Someone tied Jasper up. You might want to know how I know that."

She opened her eyes as wide as she could, pushing her head towards Charlotte.

Charlotte stifled her laughter. "Okay. Tell me how you know that."

"I let Jasper off in the morning. No one ever ties him up." Charlotte felt her stomach churn when Isla added. "Only Lester ties him up when he walks up to the hills. But I don't think he went to the hills."

"Well, Lester probably just went for a walk and didn't want Jasper to follow him. He knows he's old."

"Lester doesn't love Jasper. He hates him. I hear him say terrible things to him."

Just as she was about to ask Isla more questions the police and Alex returned to the room.

"Anything else you notice missing?" they asked.

She stood up and walked over to where the timber box that held all her precious mementos. Only a few papers and cards remained. The rest had gone with the box. She would need something else to put them in now. "I'm really upset this box has gone and nearly everything that was in there. It's not worth any money."

"You might find it tossed away at the side of the road or look in the bush nearby. Often robbers get rid of items as they leave. They work out there's nothing of any value so they throw it away."

"We'll have a good look around the place and see if we can find anything," Alex offered. "I've fixed the door latch and made sure everything locks up. You know you're welcome to stay at my place for as long as you want."

It was tempting to stay somewhere with no fear of being broken into, however she knew she'd need to come back home at some stage. There was no use putting it off. "Thanks, but I better come back here. Don't worry, I'll ring if I need."

Chapter 21

The phone woke her early the next morning. It was Alex, and after he checked how she'd slept and if everything was alright he asked if he could come and visit her that night. "I've made something special for dinner and I'd love to share it with you. Barney will mind the kids. I'd like to talk to you without them around.

She hesitated. "I'm not sure what I'm doing tonight."

"Look, I know it seems a bit unusual and not how we normally see each other, but I need some advice. I want your professional opinion on what to do about the kids' schooling. I'd really appreciate it if I could talk to you about what's best for them."

His words put her at ease. "Oh, of course. Yes, come over in the late afternoon, or whenever suits."

She'd kept herself busy during the day but every so often she felt nervous flutters in her stomach at the thought of being alone with Alex. He had that effect on her and she struggled to think straight when he was close to her. Was she imagining that his eyes rested on hers longer than needed when they talked or that he seemed to enjoy her company and conversation? She pulled a brush through her freshly washed hair, making sure she left plenty of time to get ready before he was due to arrive. Why was she so worried about how she looked? He was just coming over for some advice, not a date.

———

ALEX ARRIVED AT SUNSET, a dish full of lasagne in his hands and a bottle of red wine tucked under his arm. He had also dressed for the occasion, a white sports shirt and blue jeans, casual yet smart, his riding boots polished and clean. He had shaved and she held back a smile when she noticed the absence of stubble on his face. His voice was deep when he spoke and his gaze sent tingles across her skin. "What are you smiling about?" he asked.

Her breath caught in her throat as he bent down and kissed her on her cheek. Her words tumbled out. "Oh, nothing, well, not nothing." She laughed, breaking her nervousness. "I was just thinking that you've shaved. I'm used to seeing you with stubble on your face."

He ran his hands around his chin. "It's a special occasion. It's not every night that I get to spend some time with you, without Isla and Eli. I only got away with coming by myself because I told them I needed to talk to you about educational matters. I also said they weren't allowed to tell me what they thought was best. I just need to talk to you without their added wisdom or wants."

She took the bottle of wine from him. "It's hard to

get a word in sometimes with Isla around. She's a chatterbox."

He followed her into the kitchen where plates and cutlery were ready for the meal. "Isla talks about you constantly. The latest thing is she wants her hair to be curly just like yours."

Her hair was curled up on the top of her head and she twisted some strands of it, attempting to tuck them back into where they were supposed to be. "She'd be sorry to have this to contend with. It does its own thing." She turned around feeling a tinge of heat in her cheeks.

He studied her face for a long time. "You look lovely tonight," he murmured.

A giggle escaped her and she reminded herself to stop acting like a teenager. "Thank you. I managed to buy a new dress when I was away last week." She pressed her hands over the fabric, its small floral pattern, colourful against her skin. She looked straight up into his eyes as he took the bottle from her and poured them both a large glass of red. "Will we go out the back?" he asked. "It would be good to talk before we have dinner. I have quite a bit to run past you."

———

AS THE SUN sank behind the hills behind them, cicadas sounded from the nearby bushes. Curlews called out across the approaching darkness and Charlotte lit some kerosene heaters.

They ate their meal and talked about the day-to-day business of both their properties. Alex had quite a few mares ready to drop foals and buyers coming in from interstate to look over some of the horses. Polo events were coming up on the calendar and he was also considering staging one right here at Bindarra Creek.

Her ears pricked up. "You could use my cabins for accommodation for your guests. That's if you wanted to."

"I had thought about that. I'd love to talk about that more however what I really need is to ask you questions about the kids and their schooling."

The bottle of red was long finished and they were on their second coffee when he finally come to the decision he needed to make.

"You've just made everything clear, Charlie. I can't thank you enough. It's been so long since I've had someone to bounce ideas off. Particularly someone with a level head and inside knowledge."

"I'm not an expert on this and most of what I think you should do is just from my point of view and from someone who knows your kids a little."

"I can't believe how clear my mind is about what I need to do. I can see what is best for both Eli and Isla, and you've shown me that I'm not jeopardising their futures, but giving them much more than what they have now. Wait until I tell them that they're going to come and live with me and attend the local school."

Charlotte was excited for Alex and the kids. "I'm happy for them, but also for you. Those early years go so quickly and the kids adore you. You'd be mad to throw it all away. A good relationship with them now will carry you through the years to come."

"The bus goes right past here and like you've said, they're at a good age to change schools and both will easily make friends. They'll be country kids growing up in a small community. Once they get older, I can reassess the situation then for those high school years."

She leaned back in her chair, pleased at how animated and resolute, Alex was. "If you feel they need the larger schools in the city in the future there's plenty of time in the senior years to change them. I've called into the school here a couple of times, just out of curiosity and to say hello to the principal. She taught with someone I knew many years ago and I dropped in a parcel for her the other week. "The school is well run, has good discipline and the classes are small. The kids I met were lovely. It nearly made me want to return to teaching."

"Do you think you'll ever go back to it?"

"I have a project now with the cabins and it's a good feeling to have my own business and to build it up to how I want it."

"You seem to know exactly what you're chasing and it doesn't appear to worry you that you're doing it all by yourself, that is until your brother arrives," Alex said, a grin of amusement on his mouth. "I sense a stubborn streak in you."

"You've read me well. I think I did what someone else wanted for so long and I nearly lost sight of who I was. What a terrible thing to happen. Thank goodness I'm now my own person and living life how I want, without all the extra guff that isn't needed to be happy."

His voice was low and a soft look crossed his face. "You've taught me that. In just a short time you've made me realise what's important. It's an easy trap to fall into. Look at you and I – both of us sinking into it. At least you were young, I'm not sure what my excuse is?"

She gave him a reassuring look. "It was probably

difficult after your marriage broke up. You had two kids and I guess we clutch at what we think might make us happy."

He closed his eyes for a moment, twirling his cup in his hand. "You would have thought I would have put the two kids first, that I wouldn't have allowed Belinda to influence me as much as she did. I don't know what I was thinking."

"You need to move on. Don't look back. We all have those moments in our lives that we'd rather not think about. You've made big decisions in the last couple of weeks for both you and your kids."

He reached over and put his hand over hers. "Thank you. I mean it. Thank you."

She laughed nervously. "I haven't done anything."

"You are just yourself. When I saw you with the kids in amongst all the other guests at the party, the contrast was so distinct that it was like an epiphany, a lightning bolt that hit me. The differences in people's lives highlight how materialistic my life had become."

She squeezed his hand, a bit lost for words. "You're a wonderful dad."

It was nearly midnight by the time Alex stood up to leave. "I can't thank you enough, Charlie. I feel like my life has taken some huge turns in the last month. I wasn't thinking very clearly before." Her heart fluttered wildly as he held her hand, his lips warm on her cheek as he kissed her goodbye. They stood staring at each other, both lost for words. She shuffled her feet and pulled her hand away.

"Goodnight Alex. See you soon."

He'd stood for a bit longer, before turning and walking towards his place. Before he reached the yard gate he turned and blew her a kiss, her giggle recipro-cated by a loud chuckle as he opened the gate and walked across the paddocks.

Charlotte lay awake for hours that night, thinking of Alex and everything they had talked about. As much as she reminded herself that he was her neighbour and friend, deeper feelings were becoming stronger by the day. Tonight, she'd had the urge to stroke his arm, to sit closer to him and say that everything would be okay for the kids. She'd be there to help if he needed. She'd been mesmerised by his lips and smile, wanting to reach up and touch his face. It was like she was a teenager again, and if she didn't know better she'd think she was falling in love. Pummelling her pillow she rolled from side to side, reminding herself of all the negatives involved with relationships and men.

Outside, the wind picked up and small branches banged against the outside walls of the house. Since the break-in she wasn't at ease by herself at night, and she turned the bedside lamp on, picking up her book to read. Her eyes closed just as the sun peeped over the horizon, the book falling as she sank into a deep sleep.

Chapter 22

Charlotte woke suddenly as someone pounded on the front door. Glancing at her clock she jumped out of bed. It was nine o'clock. Usually, she was up and about by six.

"Hang on, I'll just be a minute," she called.

Pulling on a pair of shorts she twisted and knotted the side of the oversized t-shirt she always wore to bed, stumbling around, still half asleep.

When she opened the door Alex was anxiously pacing up and down the verandah.

"Is Isla here?" His voice was shaky and loud, instantly waking her from her sleepy daze.

A shiver ran through her as she looked at his distraught face. "No. Why?"

Panicked words tumbled out. "She's missing. She was there for breakfast, her plate and cup are on the table. Eli and I were up earlier and were down at the stables feeding the horses. When we came back up to the house, we couldn't find her. We've looked everywhere but there's no sign of her. I've left Eli back at the house to keep looking. I thought she might have come over here." He leaned over the verandah rails, peering over the paddocks as he phoned home again. Eli promptly answered.

"Have you found her, Eli?" he asked, jumping down the stairs and looking around the side of the house.

Charlotte could hear Eli, his voice panicky when he answered. "No, she's not here, Dad. Barney went to Auntie Bridie's house but Barney said no one was there. Their car isn't in the shed and he thought they were going into town today to get groceries."

Alex's voice was sharp. "She has to be somewhere. It's not like her to wander without Eli."

He ran down to the shed, flinging open the large gates on it, before looking up into the tree and shouting. "Isla. Isla. Just answer us, you're not in trouble."

He ran back up to Charlotte. "We've checked everywhere. The house, the stables, the yard. What about your treehouse?"

Charlotte threw on a pair of shoes. "I'll check, but you'd be able to see straight away if she was up there." I slept in this morning so I wouldn't have heard if she came for a visit. She would have knocked on my window though. Isla knows which room I sleep in." She looked into Alex's worried face. "It's not like her, is it?"

"It's not."

Charlotte put her hand on his shoulder. "She'll be here somewhere. I might go down to the paddocks towards the waterhole, just to check she didn't go that way. I don't think she would though, she'd have no reason to go there."

Alex ran a hand through his hair, his forehead creased. "I'll go back home. Keep your phone with you. We'll check everywhere again, but if we can't find her, I'll ring the police. It's not like her to wander off."

"Maybe she went with Bridie and Lester."

"I'll ring them again but Bridie would have left a note if they'd taken her. Besides she doesn't like Lester. I doubt very much she would have gone with them."

"Let's hope that's where she is." Charlotte grabbed her phone and decided not to drive, but to walk down instead. It would be quicker to go across the paddocks to the creek, plus that would be the way that Isla would have gone if she headed that way. She watched Alex sprint back across the paddocks. Please let her be at home, she thought.

Jogging slowly towards the creek she cast her eyes every way, just in case Isla was walking in one of the paddocks. The sun rose higher in the sky, the August months, cool and dry. She sidestepped as a black snake slithered through the grass in front of her. Her mind reeled at the thought that Isla would even consider walking this way alone and she checked her phone. Maybe Alex had found her. But no message or calls appeared and she quickened her pace, keeping her eyes peeled for any sign that someone had passed this way.

When she reached the creek, she called out, her shouts echoing back across the empty pools and boulders. Checking the banks for any footprints, she walked around the edges, a platypus darting back into its hideout as soon as it sighted her. There was no sign of anyone having been here. She paused and thought hard as she looked up into the heavy bush that lined the creek up the banks.

Silence thumped in her ears and her body tensed as a turtle broke the surface of the creek, its head poking out before quickly ducking back under the cover of the water. The scent of wattle bushes wafted across the water and she looked hard, making sure she hadn't missed any sign that Isla had been here.

It was unlikely that she would venture out this way by herself. And if she had, this spot was where she would be. The only other place past here were the hills and then the caves. They'd often talked about exploring them, perhaps finding the loot of bushrangers from the past. It was on their list of things to do.

Her phone rang and relief rushed through her. Alex's voice broke the silence. "I've called the police. She's not with Bridie. She just rang me back. She said Lester didn't go with her today, he was going out to fix fences instead."

Charlotte breathed heavily, her chest rising and falling as she tried to remain calm. "I'm down at the creek. She's not here and I can't see any sign that she's been this way. Alex, I'm worried she might have gone further out to the hills, even to the caves. Remember how she told us that they followed Lester across the paddocks. The kids seemed to think he was doing some-thing sneaky."

It took Alex a while to answer. "I told them both they were never to go there again or follow him. I'll talk to Eli about it. He's with Barney, looking down near the sheds."

Charlotte tried to keep her voice even. "I'm going to make my way out a bit further here. You'll probably find her there somewhere near the house, but it won't hurt to look around here a bit more. Don't panic Alex. We'll find her. Just ring me when you do."

When she hung up, a ball of fear curled in her stomach. Where else could Isla be?

Chapter 23

The track Charlotte followed, narrowed as it moved away from the more well-used paths near the rock pool. She'd only been this way for a short distance before. The caves were over a kilometre further out and it was only a rough track through the scrub after the creek. Large boulders blocked her way and she wiggled her way around them, picking up the track as it meandered its way along the creek.

Eventually, the creek filled with boulders, the water swirling through the cracks it could find. There was no going any further along the creek bank and she looked for the overgrown trail that veered off to her left. It looked like it was only used by animals. No sign of any human footprints.

Maybe she was wasting time, going in the wrong direction. Checking her phone, her body tensed as she read the "no connection" signal in the corner. When she reached the end of the bush that lined the creek she tried to ring Alex.

"Damn," she muttered. "No reception."

Should she go back and see if they had found her or go a bit further to see if there were any signs she'd been out this far?

It would be easy to find her way back; she wouldn't get lost. A cluster of branches blocked her path and she ducked her head low to climb under them, making her way through scrubby bushland, the track widening as the trees become sparser.

A flash of colour in the dirt caught her eye and she gasped. It was a pink hair tie with a bow, Isla's hair tie. Her throat tightened as she bent to pick it up. She tried her phone but again there was no reception. The ground was loose and when she looked closer at the dirt, in front of her were the small prints of a child's shoe and … she crouched down and touched them. Next to them were other footprints. They were a man's and she knew them well.

Lester's. He always wore vinyl work boots that he bought from the cheap shop. They had crisscrossed patterns on the bottom and she'd often noticed them around Alex's yard when he'd been there.

Isla must have followed him. Hopefully, she was a long way behind him and hiding behind a tree or even making her way back towards the waterhole. Charlotte quickened her pace, continually checking her phone, but to no avail. The trail petered out and she looked up as it continued through a rocky outcrop. There was no sign of Isla or footprints. Above her were three different cave openings, their caverns eerie and silent. Clambering up the rocks towards them she worried how confined the space would be inside and which one she should go into. Small tight areas had always been a problem for her. At least her phone would give her some light.

It was unlikely that Isla would enter the dark caverns by herself. She wasn't that brave. Staring at the caves, she pondered which one to enter. When she called out Isla's name there was no response and there weren't any marks that gave her a clue. She stood on the ledge, her heart in her throat as she looked around, the caves beckoning. Her head spun as she decided what to do and she peered into the first cave, the smallest opening. It didn't seem to go much further than what she could see. She shone the phone flashlight around. It was empty. The other two caves each had large entrances with a tunnel high enough for her to walk through to the back. She hesitantly entered one at a time, listening carefully before returning to the ledge.

She needed Alex and the others with her. Isla might not even have gone further and had probably headed back towards home, more than likely going back a different way. And where was Lester?

Her body tightened and she clenched her fists as she went back into the second cave. Surely Isla wasn't with Lester in there or along the tracks. She wouldn't have gone with him willingly. Nausea rose in her throat. What if he'd made her go in there? What if her instincts were right and he wasn't a good person? A decision needed to be made. If she went back and got the others it would take a couple of hours to return. If there was something sinister going on, she needed to find Isla straight away. If Isla had entered the caves to follow Lester, there was only one way out. Waiting here would be useless, but it was risky taking time and going back to get the others… she took a deep breath, Lester might hurt Isla.

A pain throbbed in her head and she rubbed her

temples. Something was drawing her into the second cave, an instinct telling her to look harder.

The bottom of the cave she stood in was covered in sand and she peered closer. At first glance it looked like no one had been this way before. There weren't any footprints or other marks that were clearly visible. Bending down she ran her fingers over the surface. The sand looked like it had been swept over, cleared, or evened, so that no signs were visible.

Questions rattled in her mind. Was it Isla who had been here and was she following Lester? Did Lester know that he was being followed?

Walking towards the back of the cave she ducked her head low before pulling out her torch. Without a backward glance she followed the tunnel into the depths of the hills.

Chapter 24

Every so often Charlotte stopped, listening for any sounds. She walked silently along the sandy path, stopping every so often to look for signs that someone had been here. The tunnel wound around and she ducked a couple of times when the ceiling came down lower, the sides narrowing and then widening as she crept further into the hillside. She glimpsed a tiny sliver of light in the distance. Perhaps the cave opened up in the hill above. She'd heard Barney talk about caves like that in the area. Maybe this one was like that.

Quickening her pace, she came to a jarring halt as a hand reached out from an alcove, strong fingers gripping her arm. She screamed and struggled, her phone falling to the ground as she wrestled with the person who appeared on her left. The barrel of a gun thrust hard into her back and she stifled a scream as a hand wrapped around her mouth.

"Stay still, you silly bitch!"

Her gut lurched as she recognised Lester's voice. When he released his hand and ordered her to turn around she stared straight into his eyes, the whites large in the light of his torch.

He pushed her forward, her legs barely carrying her, as her body shook uncontrollably.

"Shut up and don't say anything," he ordered, the butt of the gun once again pushed into her back as he propelled her along the narrow track. Trying not to stumble, she walked a short distance before the tunnel opened into a larger cave, a small camp lantern lighting up the area. Charlotte gasped loudly. Isla sat on a rock ledge, her arms crossed indignantly, her face fixed in a heavy scowl. Lester pushed Charlotte forward and she crouched next to Isla, wrapping her arms tightly around her.

Chapter 25

"It's okay Charlotte. I'm not scared,' Isla said. "Lester is just a stupid, nasty man." She dropped her voice to a whisper. "He won't shoot us. He's mean, but not that mean. We just need to run away from him, back through the tunnel and tell Dad."

'Stop talking Isla. Just be quiet for a while," Charlotte whispered.

"I came to get your treasures back," Isla continued. "I knew Lester took them. Look, he has them, plus a whole lot of other stuff. There are your binoculars and your boxes."

The nasty look that Lester threw out didn't seem to worry Isla. She gritted her teeth and glared back hard at him. "You want to watch out for that crack near your feet, Lester. You nearly walked on it when you pushed Charlotte. It's bad luck to walk on a crack. You're standing on it right now."

Lester jerked his head from side to side, looking down at the jagged crack that splintered through the rocky ground. He jumped back, and then again, ensuring he found a clear space to stand on. "No cracks now, you little smart alec." He re-checked where his feet were, wriggling back a bit further to ensure he was free of standing on any lines in the rock surface.

Isla rolled her eyes. "Your cave is not lucky. I can count thirteen big boulders in here. No wonder you want to get out of here quickly."

Lester reeled around, counting the large, rounded boulders that sat like marbles around the edge of the cave. He counted them again, his face scrunching up, fear in his eyes. Isla rolled her eyes when he growled at them.

His voice was evil. "That's why I'm out of here very soon. It might just be you and your smart mouth that will be left here with your lovely neighbour, who unfortunately has come along at the wrong time and stuffed up my plans."

Charlotte listened to the conversation between Isla and Lester. A quick glance let her know that Isla was right and Lester had some of her items that had been stolen. None of that mattered. They needed to get away from him. Isla didn't seem to be scared at all, obviously not realising the gravity of the situation. She wasn't aware of what Lester was capable of. Charlotte was though. She could see it in his eyes and his jerky movements. It was like he was on a high, running on adrenaline and focused on what he wanted to achieve. She cast her eyes around the cave. Boxes and suitcases lined the back wall of the cave, some covered in dust and cobwebs.

He squatted in the dirt in front of them, rolling a cigarette in one hand while hanging onto his gun with the other as he sneered at Isla.

"So, smarty pants. You thought you could snitch on your good old Uncle Lester. Now, look what's happened. I have the two of you here like rats in a trap. Now I just need to work out what to do with you."

Charlotte regained some of her senses, willing herself to stop shaking and to be in control for Isla's sake. "Just let us go, Lester. By the time we get back to anywhere, you can get all your stuff away. No one will know."

He laughed and she recoiled at the sight of his yellowed teeth, the gold fillings shining in the dim light. He lit his cigarette, his lips curled up in a nasty smile as he drew back and slowly blew his smoke upwards. She glanced over to the side of the cave. There was another opening, the light from the outside streaming in.

His eyebrows lifted high on his face and he followed her gaze. "Yep, that's how me and all of this is getting out of here. You've no idea what I went through to gather this." His sinister laugh echoed in the cave. "They're that stupid those coppers, they never knew where I had it. You're going to pass it all up to me in a moment. Helpers, just what I wanted.

Her voice was shaky and tears threatened to come but she willed herself to be strong. He'd love to see her cry. She knew he'd never liked her.

"Just let Isla go. She can find her way back out of the cave. Please, Lester, you don't want to be responsible for hurting a child."

He stood up, angry, waving his gun around. "It was never my intention to hurt anyone, not now or in the past. It only brings bad luck. But you stupid mongrels keep getting in my way. Now move. Pass those suitcases through the gap there. My car is there ready to go.

Nobody knows these trails except me. I'm out of here with all my stuff."

Isla helped Charlotte and together they managed to pass him up what he wanted. She saw Isla push an object to the back of the cave, pushing sand over it so he couldn't see it. She closed her eyes. Material items weren't important. Nothing was, except their lives. There was no way he was going to let them go now they'd seen all of this. She had no doubt there was worse to come.

She'd seen the tape and rope next to where Isla was when she first sat down. Her stomach heaved and bile rose in her throat. He was going to tape them up and then shoot them. She was sure of it.

Sunlight shone through the hole in the roof. A quick escape to the outside world for Lester who stood on a ladder, waving his gun around every so often, ordering them to pass items up to him. They did as they were told and Charlotte whispered reassurances to Isla as he stood above them. There was no use trying to run back out through the tunnels. He'd give chase and shoot. She'd seen him lose his temper and knew he was quick and hot-headed. It was important to try and keep him calm. A small ink drawing on the back of his neck drew her attention and she bit her lip, fear rippling through her body. It was the same tattoo of an anchor she had seen on the bank robber.

When the cave was emptied, Lester turned and waved his gun in the air, his voice terse.

"Sit back down, right where you were." Charlotte took Isla's hand and led her back to the ledge. Lester flicked his cigarette butt down and ground it into the sand with his boot. He lit another one and stood in front of them, his expression terse. Twirling his earring he looked down at his feet, moving them slightly away from a crack in the floor. He held the earring up to the light coming in through the opening, finally letting it hang down. Her heart raced as she watched him, fear overwhelming her as she thought how irrational he seemed.

Her eyes followed his movements as he reached into his pocket and pulled out a paper clipping. Charlotte gasped and recoiled as he leaned his face near to hers, his face twisted when he spoke.

"I was right. I recognised your face straight away. You thought I wouldn't remember because it was so long ago. But I'd know you anywhere." He unfolded the paper. "Famous bank robber. That's me," he snarled, his sinister grin cast towards Isla who sat stony-faced and silent.

He read out loud. "Twenty-first of August. That was a good year." He must have been engrossed in reading because he flicked the ash from his cigarette onto the dirt, taking another deep drag before continuing.

"*Local bank was held up by a man brandishing a sawn-off shotgun. Staff were terrified as he forced them to hand over the money in their tills as well as what was in the safe. A junior staff member was forced to open the safe, using numbers that she had only learned and memorised the week before.*"

He coughed and took another drag, the red embers of the end of the smoke bright in the hazy dust that filtered in through the hole above.

"Well done, my dear. Just as well, because I was that high that day and I would have probably blown your brains out if you stuffed it up."

She held her breath, guessing that he had also taken something today. He continued, "*The man took off in a white HR Holden, number plate HRQ 241. Police later located the car which had been stolen. The bags of money, the gun, and the robber have not been located. If you have any information please ring…"* Lester looked up at them, his voice dripping with sarcasm as he added, "Blah, blah, blah."

He stubbed out his smoke in the dirt before taking out a small tin and placing the butt in there. He immediately lit another cigarette and Charlotte held her breath, thinking that Isla would say what she usually did about cigarettes causing lung cancer and that he should give up. But she sat sullenly, her hand gripping Charlotte's.

Folding the paper carefully he stared at them, his look sending a shiver down her spine.

"I'm so pleased that you've kept this for all these years, my good neighbour. No one kept a copy for me. First time I've seen this." He pushed it back into his pocket. "You knew it was me, didn't you?"

She shook her head, her head tight and reeling with his accusations.

"And, you knew it was me when you served me at another bank. If I didn't know better I'd think that you've been following me around. Stalking me." He twirled his earring around a few times, closing his eyes almost like he was in a trance.

Suddenly he pointed his gun at her, his sickly voice changing to an angry, volatile tone. "Who knows where you two are? Does anyone else know? Do I need to do this quickly and get out of here before anyone else comes?"

Isla spoke up, her eyes looking straight at Lester. "I told a lie. I left a note and said I had gone to the shops and hairdressers with Bridie. Dad won't worry about me until Bridie gets back home from town."

He grinned. "Clever girl. That's good work. She won't be back until this afternoon. Going to get her hair done and see her stupid friends. And what about you?"

Charlotte tried to keep her voice even. "I often walk to the creek. I never knew that anyone else came this way. I've been wanting to explore the caves for ages. It's just that I found Isla's hair tie near the creek and I was worried that she'd walked off somewhere by herself." She pulled the tie out of her pocket to back up her story. "I was worried that she might get lost and I wasn't sure if any of the others were with her, so I thought I'd have a look around. I never expected to find her and all of this."

"Or me?"

The three of them sat in silence and she could tell he was trying to work out what to do.

Isla piped up. "I don't think it's a good idea that you shoot us. I've seen that on television and no matter how you do it there would be a lot of blood. You hate blood. You told Eli that, and how it would bring a curse on him when he squashed the mozzie on his arm and the blood splattered everywhere. If you shoot us, you'll remember it for the rest of your life. You'll be like the man in the murder book who couldn't sleep ever again in the dark for the rest of his life because every time he shut his eyes blood would drip down and he was cursed and the blood was always there. It dripped on everything, every-where, drip, drip, drip. When he ate food, drip, drip, drip, it tasted like blood and drip …"

"Shut up!" Lester roared. "You, Miss Bank Girl, tape her up and make sure you do her mouth first. I've been waiting to shut her up for ages." His eyes flitted from side to side, his movements and words jerky and agitated. Charlotte wished Isla had kept quiet but she should have known sooner or later the words she found so easily would flow.

As she taped Isla's mouth, hands, and feet she whispered, "Just stay quiet. Don't make him angrier. We'll be alright." She tried to do it loosely but Lester checked and at one stage ripped the tape from her hands and bound it tighter. Isla whimpered, her eyes moving back and forth as she watched Lester do the same to Charlotte.

Charlotte's legs shook uncontrollably when Lester picked up the lengths of rope beside Isla. He used them to tie them both up, twirling the rope around them several times, making sure they weren't able to move. The tight cord cut into her skin but she kept her eyes fixed on Isla's, trying to hold her gaze instead of watching Lester.

He cast his eyes around the cave. "I've got what I came for and," he pushed his face right up close to Isla's, "I had no intention of shooting either of you. That's too quick and bloody. My loot has been here for over fifteen years and no one has ever come into this cave. It's on private land, so no walkers or tourists ever come this way. The rough track I've cut in from the other side is only known to me and I've covered every trace of us coming in here. It should be another fifteen years before anyone ever looks around here or finds their way in here."

He sneered at them. "A natural slow death doesn't count for bad luck." He touched his earring again, stepping carefully over the cracks. As he took one last look around, his unhinged laughter echoed through the cave. "Adios, my friends," he jeered. As he climbed the ladder and pulled it up behind him Charlotte tried to use her eyes to silently plead with Isla. *Lie still, don't struggle.* She willed her not to move. Isla lay motionless, her body curled up into a ball as tears rolled down her cheeks.

Charlotte listened carefully for the sounds above. It sounded like he had filled his car with the items from the cave and her stomach sank as she watched branches being laid across the narrow opening. He was right. No one would find them. She had only said she was going to the creek. No one would suspect they had come this far.

The light faded as the branches completely blocked the opening into the hillside and she listened to the sound of his car, the rough ground above crunching under the tyres. She listened until she couldn't hear the car any longer.

Chapter 26

Charlotte's throat was dry and she tried to wriggle closer to Isla, but Lester had bound the tape and ropes tightly, and as much as she tried there was no way she could escape. How many days could a person survive like this, with no water or food? What about when they needed to go to the toilet? Tears rolled down her face and she pushed her shoulder up against Isla's leg, trying to give her some comfort.

Darkness crept into the cave and the air cooled as night fell. Before she fell asleep she took one last look up at the night sky, just visible through the cover of branches that Lester had placed over the opening.

A scratchy sound woke her up, a noise in the tunnel they had entered through. Nausea rose in her throat and her body stiffened as she imagined Lester returning. When she closeted her body around Isla's, the little girl pushed her legs closer to Charlotte, both drawing strength from each other as they lay and listened to the noises. Charlotte's mind raced and she struggled against her ties. Maybe Lester had changed his mind and was coming back to finish them off.

When a tongue licked her face she jerked her head back in fear. Opening her eyes in the darkness she could make out the shape of Jasper. He barked and Isla moved beside her. His loud barks echoed in the cave and he pushed her with his nose before lying down beside them, his head resting on her arm. He was puffing and she nudged him, knowing that he often slept for hours after even a short walk. After she pushed him harder with her body, his face nuzzled hers. Grunting from behind the tape she tried to get him to move. Isla did the same, squirming and moving around, trying to will him to go and get help.

Jasper eventually moved away, walking slowly around the edge of the cave before ambling off back through the tunnel. He came back again and peered at them from the opening before disappearing. Charlotte let her body go limp, her legs and arms aching from the position she was in. Lester had known what he was doing and even when she struggled against the ties they remained tight on her skin. There was no way of telling the time but she guessed that a couple of hours had passed since Jasper first arrived. The dog must have followed her and found his way into the caves. Thank goodness he hadn't arrived while Lester was still there. Goodness knows what he would have done with him. The trouble was Jasper had probably only walked back out as far as the first cave before lying down again. She couldn't imagine that he would make it much further than that.

Her heart pounded hard and she closed her eyes,

trying to remain calm and think of what else she could do. Her arms and legs ached and she thought about how worried Alex and the others would be. They'd come looking along the creek and then maybe search a bit further afield. Perhaps they would find their way to the caves. The trouble was they would have no reason to go any further. She'd only found the openings because of Isla's hair tie. There was nothing to suggest that anyone had entered any further. They would have no reason to think like that.

Suddenly Jasper was back, his tongue on her face again, forcing her to open her eyes. Isla wriggled up next to her, her tiny face pushed into her chest. The dog disappeared again. Charlotte's chest tightened and her body ached as the hopelessness of the situation pressed down on her. Suddenly she glimpsed a sliver of light on one side of the cave wall. The light got brighter and larger and her body shivered, terrified of who was coming. Jasper appeared again, his sharp barks resounding through the cave as he lay down next to her. A bright light appeared behind him and she gasped as she looked up, straight into the wide eyes of Barney, who peered down at her and Isla, a flood of tears streaming down his face.

ALEX AND ELI removed the tape and ropes from them. Barney sat down on one of the boulders, his head between his hands as he tried to regain his breath. "I'll be alright. It's just a bit of a shock to come across you both like this. Don't worry about me, just keep rubbing your arms and legs to get the blood circulating."

"Please don't cry, Barney. Charlotte found me and Lester has gone." Isla's voice was raspy and Charlotte passed her some water. 'I want to go to sleep,' she said. 'I don't want to be a detective anymore. My arms and legs hurt."

Eli hugged her. "Thank goodness Jasper found you both."

When Isla looked up at him her eyes were wide. "Lester's stupid. He walked under that tall ladder he has propped against the wall. He kept going under it when he was angry with us and trying to decide what to do. Even I know that's bad luck." Reaching over she picked up something from the ground. "And when he grabbed that tape from Charlotte, his arm scraped across the rock." She held the object high in the air for a second before letting it drop to the ground. "Lucky four-leaf-clover. See you later."

Alex had hardly spoken since he'd entered the cave and Charlotte could see he was in shock. When he'd rubbed her arms and shoulders his face had been stricken with worry as he looked from her to Isla.

"I'm okay. Just worry about Isla," she'd assured him as they looked around the cave one more time. "Just get us out of here. I want to get out." She'd tried to keep her voice even but an overwhelming worry that Lester might come back rattled her.

Alex bent down to get something from under the sand that Isla pointed to. Thank goodness she was okay and Lester hadn't hurt her before she got there.

Eli took her arm and she followed him and Barney, Jasper right beside her as they made their way back out through the tunnel. Every so often she turned to make sure Alex and Isla were behind her. They all needed to get out safely, through the tunnels, across the paddocks, and through the gate to home.

Chapter 27

Charlotte tried to remain stoic as they trekked back out to the cave where she had originally entered. Alex checked on her continually, his strong arms wrapped around Isla as she clung to him. Their pace was slow and they stopped every so often to give Jasper a rest. By the time they made their way along the creek and out into the open paddocks the light had disappeared from the sky.

In the distance an ambulance and two police cars, waited for them at the gate. She declined a ride in the ambulance. "Take Isla. Alex can go with her. I promise you I'm fine. Barney and Eli will come with me in the police car. I hope Jasper will fit in." The two police officers ensured Jasper was settled at their feet before the vehicles made their way back through the gate, past Charlotte's house, and onto the lane that led to Alex's place.

She didn't have the strength to question where they were going. Her mind was numb and all she wanted to do was lie down and sleep. A strong cup of tea and sandwiches that the police officer made them all, helped her regain some strength and she watched in amazement as Isla ate voraciously, her little face lighting up in a wide grin when the police officer produced a packet of chocolate biscuits.

The ambulance staff left after talking to her. Apart from a few red marks where the tape had cut into her skin, physically, she was fine. Two other detectives arrived and the rest of the night blurred into a succession of questions and paperwork. Barney hugged her before leaving to go back to his place, his kind eyes still teary when he spoke. "We thought we'd lost both of you. That area is a maze of tunnels and tracks. If it wasn't for old Jasper here, well…"

"I know Barney. We're very lucky and I'll remember the look on your face for the rest of my life." Her voice shook and he'd stopped her from talking, his hand patting her shoulder as he said goodbye.

Alex had seen Barney to the door before coming back to sit next to her. "I've put Isla to bed. Eli has placed a mattress on the floor next to her and he'll sleep there in case she wakes up during the night. He suggested it. I was going to bring her to bed with me but she wanted to go in her own bedroom with her dolls and books so I've let him be her protector for the night."

She nodded, lost for words, her head pounding after the events of the day.

The police asked a few more questions. "We might leave this for now. We've got all the information that we need and there are alerts out for this area as well as the rest of the state. The other stations have been notified and we're hoping someone spots him before he causes any more trouble."

"Do you think he'll come back here?" Charlotte asked, her fear rising at the thought of ever seeing Lester again.

"We highly doubt it. We're going to leave two officers here though. They'll be positioned in cars so that they'd see him if he came from any direction. I wouldn't worry too much though, we've already had a report from a petrol station a few hours from here. We think he's headed west."

Alex saw them to the door, making sure that everything was locked up and secure. He came back to her. "I want you to stay here until they catch him. No arguments, please. I won't be able to sleep unless you're here safe with us."

She breathed a quiet sigh of relief. "Thank you."

"You can use the same bedroom as last time. There are fresh towels in the bathroom and the policewoman took the liberty of getting some clothes from your house while you were having something to eat.

"Oh, thank goodness. I just want to have a shower and get out of these clothes."

He passed her a small bag. "I just asked her to grab some underwear and a few pieces of clothing for you."

She looked into the bag, her voice barely audible. "Thank you."

He smiled as if reading her thoughts. "How about you freshen up and get some sleep. We'll have plenty of time to talk about everything in the morning. It's late." She stood up next to him, his hand reaching out to push some straggling hairs back from her face. Tears sprung to her eyes and she willed them back, her words stuck when she went to speak.

When she lifted her eyes to meet his gaze, he pulled

her gently towards him, pressing her close to the warmth of his body. She let herself be drawn in, laying her head on his chest as he held her tight. The stress of the day drained from her body as his strong arms wrapped around her. When she finally pulled back their eyes met and he bent down and kissed her on the forehead. Her skin tingled where his lips had been, his words soft when he spoke. "Go to bed, Charlie. I'll see you in the morning."

A warm shower helped sleep come quickly, although she'd tossed and turned throughout the night. In the morning she rose early, looking out the window.

The police officers were in the yard talking to Alex. They'd driven off not long after and by the time she got to the kitchen he was back inside, sitting with Eli and Isla who were having their breakfast.

Isla jumped up and hugged her, putting her hands around Charlotte's face and squeezing her cheeks. "You saved me. You and Jasper and Dad and Barney and Eli, you all saved me."

Alex pried Isla away. "Let Charlie sit and have some breakfast."

Eli also gave her a long hug. "Dad said you're going to stay here with us for a while at night. He said when you go home during the day I'm to go with you and look out for you."

She pulled a chair out and smiled, casting a quizzical look Alex's way. "Did he now? Well, it does sound like a plan."

Alex served her a meal of bacon and eggs that he had prepared and left warming in the oven. The aroma of crispy bacon made her mouth water and she realised how hungry she was. Yesterday she'd only eaten a quick breakfast and then the sandwiches she'd been given last night. She ate quickly, listening to Alex and the children as they went over the events of the past day. Isla didn't seem fazed at all although she promised them all that she would never venture further than the gate without any of them.

When the children finished eating Alex asked them to go to the stables and check on the two mares who were ready to drop their foals. She listened to them as they left, Isla as usual talking non-stop, filling in Eli on every little detail from yesterday.

"She's a tough cookie," Charlotte said, washing down the breakfast with a glass of freshly squeezed orange juice that Eli made for her.

Alex had stubble on his cheeks this morning and dark rings under his eyes. It was obvious he hadn't slept much and she watched him as he moved around the room, before returning to sit next to her with a fresh cup of coffee.

"She is, but she doesn't realise the seriousness of what could have happened. It sounds like it was only Lester's paranoid state of mind about superstitions that stopped him from harming both of you."

"You know Isla never let him see that she was scared. It wasn't until after he left and she was next to me that I could tell she was really frightened." Her words caught in her throat. "She didn't like being tied up."

Alex reached over and placed his hand on her arm. "I didn't sleep at all last night. I spent most of the time checking on her and Eli.' He looked down. "I have to be honest, I even opened your door a little and checked that you were okay. Your lamp was still on but you were fast asleep."

A tight feeling in her chest made her take a deep breath. "Thank you. I don't think what happened has sunk in yet."

Alex's fingers stroked her arm, his touch warm and reassuring. "I kept thinking about what could have happened to both of you and how I should have done something about Lester a long time ago. I should have followed my gut instincts."

"You weren't to know. Who knew that he had been hiding all that stuff for so long and that he had a gun?"

"I've never seen that gun before. He must have had it hidden because Bridie tells me she never knew he had it either. She said she wouldn't have allowed him to have it on the property."

"How is Bridie?"

"She's distraught. Not about him leaving but about what he did to you and Isla. She's in at the police station for questioning today but she said she's going to go to her daughter's place for a while. She feels responsible and doesn't think that I'll trust her with the kids ever again."

They chatted for a long while and it was comforting to talk about what had happened. The police had been interested in her previous connections to Lester and praised her for keeping her cool and not antagonising him further. It didn't however make the hollow feeling in her stomach go away. Her nerves were still on edge and a heavy feeling pressed down on her. Later that day when she returned to her house with Eli and Barney in tow, she'd only wanted to grab a few more clothes before heading back to Alex's place. At the moment it was the only place she felt safe. Her head whirred with crazy thoughts about Lester returning. It would be easy for him to come back to find her and make sure this time she didn't get away. She and Isla had nearly ruined his plans and she didn't believe that he would just go and forget about them. Once he found out that they had been rescued it might be likely that he would secretly return and pay her back for what had happened.

He would be on the run and it wouldn't take him long to work out the police were tracking him. Lester would blame her. She felt it with all her soul. His super-stitions would be thrown out the window because now he'd have nothing to lose. He would seek vengeance.

Chapter 28

For the next few days, Charlotte felt as if she was floating through time. Nothing seemed to matter anymore and she kept asking herself why she wasn't interested in anything. Alex prompted her with questions about her plans for the retreat. When were her guests arriving and her brother?

"I'm not sure if I should have the guests come. Jacob will come soon. I've spoken to him and my parents. I glossed over the events of the last few days a bit. I don't want them to worry. I'll tell them the full story when I see them in person."

Hours drifted past as she spent the days sleeping. For some reason, she seemed to have no energy and just wanted to shut her eyes and forget about the fact that Lester was still out there somewhere. Other times she wandered down to the stables, noting that Eli and Isla were never far from Alex, with Barney also close by.

She did look forward to dinner, which Alex always cooked. Barney ate with them and Jasper lay on the mat just inside the door. The men made sure to keep the conversation light and Eli kept them entertained with his funny stories from boarding school. Any topic other than Lester and the caves.

Isla had been a bit quieter than usual for the first couple of days. Alex confided in her. "She's been having some nightmares. The last two nights she's ended up in my bed. I'm surprised you haven't heard her getting up or putting the lights on."

"I've slept heavily. It's not making me any less tired during the day though."

When a new foal was born, Isla was kept busy helping to keep an eye on it. The mare was not in good health and the vet made numerous visits. Help was needed looking after the foal. It was excellent timing and kept Isla busy. When she wasn't busy in the stables she clung to Alex and most of the time could be found holding his hand or hoisted onto his shoulders as he went about his daily work.

Charlotte needed to return to her house, but panic filled her every time she thought of being there by herself. She might ring Jacob and ask him to come and visit. She didn't want to outstay her welcome at Alex's place, although he didn't seem to mind her being there. She also didn't want to put Jacob out. Everyone had their own lives and she needed to get on with hers. She couldn't live in this bubble forever. Tonight at dinner would be a good time to tell Alex and the kids.

They'd not long sat down and she bided her time, waiting for the right moment. Alex jumped up to answer the phone. It was the local constable. Alex nodded as he listened, an occasional, "okay", or "I see", the only response. All eyes turned toward him as they waited for him to return to the table.

His face was drawn as he sat down and looked around the table at them. Isla sat next to him and he wrapped his arm around her shoulder, giving her a gentle squeeze. "They've found Lester. His car went off the side of one of the ranges down near the South Australian border. The road was wet and they said he was travelling too fast. He's dead."

Charlotte held her breath while the two children sat with their eyes wide and mouths open. Alex looked at her, his face drawn with concern. "Are you okay?"

She bit her lip, trying not to cry with the relief from what she had heard. "I'm okay." Eli kept blinking and she reached over and squeezed his arm. "It's okay, Eli. It's okay to not feel sad about it."

When Eli stood up and hugged her, she realised how much he'd matured over the last week. "I feel like I do when my team wins the football. I feel like we've won yet Lester is dead and you shouldn't feel happy about that."

"This is different," Charlotte explained. "We all feel a bit happy and relieved because now we don't ever have to look over our shoulders or worry about him coming back to…" she stopped and looked over at Isla, "…we don't want him to come back and annoy us, do we Isla."

Isla sat up straight, her innocent blue eyes bright, as everyone waited for her to speak. "He should never have walked under that ladder. I knew when he did that he was going to not have a good ending and that we would be okay. It would have been okay if we walked under it because we aren't crazy about superstitions like he is. But it was not good for him."

Alex threw Charlotte an amused glance. "You are two smart kids and we're all lucky that Charlie was here to help save the day. Now about Lester, well, good riddance to bad rubbish. That's all I got to say. Now we all need to get on with our lives. There's no use letting a mongrel like that ruin your life. The main thing is everyone is okay and we're all here together."

Charlotte's eyes brimmed with tears as they raised their glasses and clinked them together. Isla wriggled in her chair, as usual jumping quickly to another topic. "Dad, can I give the foal a name?"

He smiled widely. "You certainly can."

"I want to name it Charlie, after Charlotte. Because she's a hero."

He winked at Charlotte. "That's a great name."

"Oh no, please don't do that Isla. Think of something else. All I've done is brought trouble to everyone." She stood up, unable to hold the tears back. Wiping them away with the back of her hand she managed to talk, her voice uneven. "I think I'll go to bed. Tomorrow I'll need to go back to my place. Thanks for dinner, Alex."

She rushed back to her room and closed the door behind her. A heaviness pressed down on her chest and she curled up and pulled the covers over herself. She needed to be alone, to not have to talk to anyone or to put on a brave face in front of the children anymore. She couldn't do it. She just wanted to sleep and not have to face anyone. Alex and Barney were too kind. If she hadn't talked about the caves or said she missed her stolen items, Isla would never have gone to the cave or followed Lester.

WHEN CHARLOTTE CAME DOWNSTAIRS the following morning, everyone was already outside. She could see the kids going back and forth from the stable. Thank goodness the foal was giving them something else to think about. She'd collect her belongings and once she had something to eat she'd head for home. Maybe once she was back there, she'd regain her energy and motivation. At the moment she had nothing. Nothing to give and nothing she wanted. Just a numbness that pressed down heavy on her.

"Oh, you're finally up. We thought we'd let you sleep." Alex caught her by surprise as he appeared through the side door.

She flicked the jug on. "I'm just making a cup of tea and then I'll go home. You've been more than kind to let me stay here but I need to go back and sort everything out."

He stared at her and she looked down at the floor, not wanting to meet his gaze.

"Are you okay?" he asked, his voice soft.

She tried to force a smile. "Yes, yes. I'm fine. I just need to get back into routine."

"The kids will miss you here. Isla has bounced back way better than I thought she would."

"She's only little. Her mind doesn't work like an adult, imagining all that could have been."

He put out his hand and rested it on her arm. "Charlie, don't shut me out. I know it's been rough but I'm here for you."

Her mind froze and her body tensed. Her dad and Jacob had always called her Charlie. Aunt Lucille had started it and when she was a kid it had been her nick-name. Now it brought memories flooding back. Good years, fun times as kids with a loving family and a beautiful aunt who had meant the world to her.

What had happened? Her marriage had busted up, she'd lost Aunt Lucille and now she'd nearly managed to get herself and Isla killed by a crazy person. Everything was spiralling downwards, and the tears once again threatened to come. She willed them back. The last thing she wanted was sympathy.

She pulled her arm away. "That's the most important thing, that Isla is doing well. That's all that matters."

"You matter also. You're not yourself and last night you talked as if some of what happened was your fault. I don't think you're thinking straight."

Her chest heaved up and down and she folded her arms.

"Why do you think Isla went to the caves. I'd said the week before we should go and explore them. She went to get my stuff back because I said I missed a couple of things. I'd encouraged them to be free and explore, to be independent and brave. Look what happened. Of course, It's my fault. You had strict rules before the kids knew me. They wouldn't have dared to go beyond that gate. My reckless attitude inspired Isla to do what she did. She would never have gone there otherwise."

Alex held out his arms and tried to wrap them around her. She gently pushed them away as he frowned at her.

"That's ridiculous. You're not thinking properly. This all happened because Lester is a criminal. Because he was a crazy person who wanted to take all his money and destroy anyone who knew about it or was going to stand in his way."

She picked up her bag and stared up into his eyes. "I overstepped the mark with your kids. Never again. Isla could have been killed, all because of what I'd told them. I need to go home."

He gripped both her arms, anger in his voice. "I don't want to hear that rubbish. You're completely wrong. You need to snap out of the way you're thinking. What happened to carefree, brave Charlotte who we all admire?"

She wiped her hand over her face, the tears falling down her cheeks. "I was wrong. I'm going home."

Chapter 29

Alex stayed away for a couple of days. He'd sent Barney and the kids over with some food and a bunch of flowers. They'd woken Charlotte from where she lay on the lounge, dirty dishes scattered on the coffee table and a row of mugs unwashed from the copious cups of coffee she'd drunk. The television had some stupid sitcom playing on it and Eli had turned it off as soon as he entered the room.

"You always told us not to waste time watching television," Eli said, picking up the cups and taking them to the kitchen. Isla curled up beside her while Jasper lay on the floor next to the lounge. She put her hand out to pat the top of his head, rewarded with a lick from him before he laid down, his soft snoring making Isla giggle.

Barney sat on one of the lounge chairs, his eyes roaming along the line of paintings.

"Maybe we should do some painting this week," he suggested, "or do you have to get the cabins ready for the guests coming next month?"

She wrapped her arms around Isla. "They've

cancelled. I'm not sure if they heard about what happened on the news or if they were telling the truth when they said they had family problems and couldn't come. They wouldn't let me refund the deposit. They said they'd come at another time."

"What about your parents and Jacob?"

"I've been on the phone to them every day. Dad has to go in for a hernia operation. I want Jacob to stay there and drive Mum around and make sure everything is okay. I've assured them I'm fine and there is nothing they can do. They'll come for a visit once Dad is out and recovered."

Barney made that funny hmph noise he liked to make when he disagreed with something.

"I'm okay Barney. Just tired that's all."

"Well, I'm coming here tomorrow and I want to paint. The kids will be back at school before we know it, so it would be fun to have an art day for all of us."

She closed her eyes. "I don't really feel like painting."

"Please, please," Isla put her hands on Charlotte's face, pushing her cheeks tightly, out and then in.

For once it didn't make her laugh. It didn't make her angry either, or sad, just nothing.

Eli came back into the room. "We can come over at nine. I'll set the easels up and get the paints ready. I know where they all are in the shed. We'll do it on the back verandah."

"Righto," Barney said as he stood up. "Nine o'clock it is. Be ready with your artist clothes on."

Isla snuggled in before planting a sloppy kiss on Charlotte's face. Jumping up she grabbed Barney's hand, her voice excited and bubbly. "Painting, nine o'clock. Be there or be square."

———

CHARLOTTE SLEPT IN AGAIN. She couldn't be bothered setting an alarm and the banging on the back door woke her from a deep sleep. When she stuck her head out the window, both kids and Barney waved to her from the verandah.

"Start setting up, I'll be out there soon," she murmured.

A short dress and old jumper hung loose on her. She'd lost weight. It was only ten days since Isla had gone missing but she hadn't eaten much since. Food was the last thing she felt like.

She'd tried to act enthusiastic and happy about the painting day. The kids had brought food and cold drinks and she'd spread out a blanket on the verandah where they sat and had lunch. Barney perched on an old wooden chair, telling them stories about the horse and foals he'd reared when he was young. He'd grown up in the Armidale area and recalled times of freezing winters and flooding rains, of summers that were so hot and dry, that the dams and creeks had dried up. He marvelled about autumns that turned the town red and orange, the fallen leaves from the deciduous trees that lined every street turning the ground into a colourful carpet.

The scenes he conjured up were the perfect view to paint. Rocky plains with meandering bubbling brooks cutting their way through the outcrops of rocks and tufts of grass like what she'd seen when she'd driven down from the coast or gone exploring. But the colours didn't go the way she wanted and her bubbling brooks looked like straight rivers of brown. In the end she'd scrunched the paper up and thrown it in the bin. You had to be in the right frame of mind to paint and she just wasn't.

She lay on the day bed and watched the others. Barney was a masterful artist and she was astounded by the skill of his brushwork, the way he applied the paint and the technique he used with the lines and shades that brought the picture to life. Eli had also done a few small pieces. He worked quickly and the last one he completed in half an hour. It was an intricate pencil drawing of Charlotte lying on the daybed, Jasper at her feet curled up, his nose resting on her feet. Both had their eyes closed.

Isla spent the entire time drawing foals. She also was quite artistic and as Charlotte told her, it wasn't easy to draw animals. Practice was what she needed.

When they finished they rested on the verandah next to where Charlotte lay, watching the horses in the paddocks beyond the house. She hadn't felt very talk-ative and besides who needed to talk when Isla was around. It was easier to listen as she and Eli chatted about what their new school would be like, who their teachers were going to be and what kids they'd met before they even went there.

"We're going to meet new friends and lots of kids who live not far from here. The teachers already know we're coming and they've got buddies for us to show us around," Isla stood up to talk and waved her hands around wildly to demonstrate how big the school was and how many friends she was going to make.

Eli was also excited about going to the local school. "The best part is that Dad can come and watch us play sport and we just catch the bus home in the afternoon and it will stop right at the front gate."

"It's just us and Dad now. No more Belinda and no more Lester," Isla added.

"It will be so much fun. I can't wait to hear all about it next time I see you." She'd hugged them all as they prepared to go home, assuring Barney again that she was okay. He'd given her that look, a disgruntled frown and she knew he was not happy with her. "I'm just in a slump," she assured him. "I'm fine."

Chapter 30

Alex rang a couple of days later. "Just checking on you. I thought you might have called in to see the kids. They have a lot to tell you about school. They've been in for some of the holiday open days. You know, lots of fun activities and meet and greet everyone."

She tried to sound happy, but her voice was flat. "I'll catch up with them soon. I've been busy."

He knew her too well. "Doing what?"

"Oh, you know. This and that." It was of course a lie. Most days she didn't get out of bed until late. She'd sit for hours on the verandah looking across the paddocks. Then she'd sleep some more. Reading and listening to music annoyed her and made her irritated. She didn't have any inspiration to paint or garden, or even to continue with her renovations on the cabins. She had nothing.

"Well, I hope you're out of bed because I've just dropped the kids off at a soccer day at the school so I'm calling in. I won't stay long. I have something for you."

The phone call made her clean the kitchen. The last

thing she wanted was for Alex to know she hadn't done the dishes for days or that there wasn't much to eat in the pantry or fridge. If she had everything out ready, he wouldn't need to go in there. She set the table on the verandah ready for a cuppa, did her hair, and put on some clean clothes.

Her heart thumped hard when she watched him get out of the car. His face was freshly shaven and he wore jeans, a T-shirt, and his riding boots. His arms and legs were tanned and muscled and he looked relaxed and happy as he kissed her cheek, in his hand a large paper bag that he placed on the table.

"Come and sit," she said, gesturing to the chairs.

"How have you been, Charlie? I feel like I haven't seen you for ages."

"I'm fine. You know, just keeping busy around here."

"I've brought something for you. Isla remembered something about the day you were in the cave and she thought that it might make you feel "not sad", her words."

"She's thoughtful. Chocolate?"

"Not quite." He pulled the object out of the bag. "She said she hid it when Lester took the other stuff up the ladder to his ute."

He handed Charlotte the timber box that her father had made her. The one that had been full of her mementos, that were now, who knew where. Lester's ute had caught fire and the police said there wasn't anything left they could save.

She bit her lip, running her fingers over the smooth surface. "This means a lot to me. If there was anything that I wanted to get back it would have been this." She looked up into his concerned eyes. "He could have killed us both. I'll never understand why he didn't."

"Too superstitious. He always has been. We used to leave our riding boots up on the table in the stable and he'd swipe his hand across the lot and fling them to the ground. Poor Bridie lived under a whole set of his stupid rules, all based on superstitions. He went nuts one night because she brought the washing in after dark. He said she'd bring the devil in with it."

"Maybe she did."

He leaned forward. "He already had the devil in him. Some people are just born bad."

Memories flooded back as she looked over the paddocks.

Alex's words broke her thoughts. "You have to get on with life, Charlie. Put this behind you. If you're not able to, you should go and talk to someone. A professional. You know it's been offered to you several times. Just go and get some help on how to deal with what happened. Sometimes events are too big for us to deal with ourselves."

She wanted to cry, to howl like a kid, and wash away all the unhappiness that pressed down on her. This wasn't her. She'd been through so many other calamities and always managed to get through without any help from anyone else. She just wanted to feel happy again.

She could feel Alex's eyes on her as she ran her hands over the box. Slowly she opened the lid. The inside was like she was, empty. Nothing left, nothing emotional or reminiscent of what her life had been. All the little notes and cards were now ashes, any remnant of her past life, swiped off the side of the range with Lester.

She gathered her thoughts, trying to keep her mind even and not let Alex know she was having trouble coping. She mustered a smile. "I'm doing okay. Thank Isla for the box. She's one in a million. Is she okay?"

"Kids are resilient. I keep an eye on her and Eli but they are that excited about starting at the local school, plus the foal arriving they seem to have forgotten about what happened. Isla was even okay going today without me. I offered to stay but she said she had made some friends and Eli was there so I wasn't to worry. They've had plenty to keep them occupied. The only thing they're worried about is you."

She stood up. "Tell them I'm doing great. They can come to visit whenever they want."

He stood next to her. "The kids tell me you just lie on the day bed and watch them. That you don't play with them anymore and you won't paint."

She pushed her hair behind her ears. Even though she'd brushed it before Alex arrived it was always so straggly and curly. It probably looked like she hadn't brushed it for days. "I just need some vitamins or something. I am a bit tired. I'll buy some when I'm in town next."

He picked up the cups and followed her into the kitchen. She wasn't able to stop him quick enough and he picked up the milk and put it back in the fridge. Thank goodness he didn't say anything. He must not have noticed that there wasn't much food in there. She really needed to go to town and buy some groceries.

Her arms and legs felt heavy and she leaned on the kitchen bench, listening to him as he talked about the horses and what was going on in the polo world. After a while he stopped. "Sorry to talk so much. You don't seem that interested."

She stood up and folded her arms. "I'm sorry, Alex. I'm just not in the mood for talking."

He reached out for her hands but she kept her arms crossed and looked down.

Stepping away from her, he smiled. "We'll see you soon, Charlie. Don't be a stranger. Come and see the kids and the foal."

"Will do," she answered.

Chapter 31

Several days passed and as much as Charlotte tried she couldn't break out of whatever slump she was in. There was no way she was going to talk to a doctor or anyone. There was nothing wrong with her, she was just feeling a bit down. You weren't supposed to feel happy all the time, wasn't that what everyone kept saying?

Tomorrow, Jacob and her parents were arriving. She'd been surprised when they rang. Her father was doing fine and they thought they'd come for a drive to get him out of the house. They'd only stop a couple of days, but Jacob might stick around for a while.

"Finally," she thought. Jacob was like her other half. Once he arrived, she'd feel better. She wondered why all of a sudden he was able to come. Perhaps work had given him holidays. It wouldn't have anything to do with the Lester incident. She'd never gone into details and from talking to Mum she could tell they didn't have any idea how close she had come to not seeing them again.

She lay on the daybed, going over the events of that day. If only she had let Alex know her suspicions earlier, or not encouraged the kids to be so free-range. Her heart pounded and she wondered if this was what a panic attack felt like or if it was just her nerves on edge. She'd been having nightmares every night, the house echoed and felt empty and cold. Some nights she was sure she could hear noises outside. She took deep breaths. Lester was dead. There was no reason to be scared anymore.

She sat up and looked over the paddocks, the only other house in sight was Alex's. Maybe living here in an isolated place was not such a good idea. Perhaps she needed to go back to the city, to the coast, where neighbours were closer and things like robbers hiding their treasure in old bushranger's caves didn't happen.

Maybe this had all been a mistake. A reflex action she'd taken without thinking too much after her marriage breakup. Her eyes roamed over the house and garden. The cabins were a bonus to the property. She'd be able to sell easy enough. Prices were good in the area and she had made some improvements and spruced the place up a bit.

She lay back down. It seemed like a good decision. A move back to Queensland would be easy. Perhaps go back to teaching. There were always plenty of jobs and she could throw herself into work, spend her time with kids and get back into the routine of work. Her eyes felt heavy and she let herself sink back into the saggy old mattress. Sleep. It made her feel better.

Chapter 32

Charlotte made an effort to look good the day her family arrived. She didn't realise how much weight she'd lost until she put on her floral dress. It hung baggy on her, her arms and legs thinner. Her hair had lost its usual shine and she tied it up high on her head. Some makeup and lip gloss would help. At least her arms and legs were still tanned, her face looking somewhat healthy.

Her mother noticed straight away. "Oh my God, Charlie. You're wasting away. How much weight have you lost?"

Jacob rolled his eyes and embraced her in a bear hug. When he pulled away, he also looked her up and down, checking out her thin legs. Dad was still recovering from his operation and walked slowly up the stairs and into the loungeroom. She made sure he was settled on the lounge before she gave the other two a tour of the property.

Jacob loved it. The paddocks, the sheds, and the cabins.

"So much potential. I'm sorry I didn't get down earlier. But now I'm here for a while."

"Well, actually I need to talk to you about that."

The two of them wandered off towards the creek, leaving Mum to sit with Dad and relax. The drive had taken it out of him a bit.

She filled Jacob in on what had happened the day that Isla went missing. When they reached the rock pool she stood for a long while staring into the depths of the dark water. "I haven't been here since it happened. I don't think it's actually sunk in yet."

"You made out it was nothing. If I'd known it was that bad, I would have come straight down. Why didn't you tell me?"

There was so much going on with Mum and Dad and you were trying to sort out your own life. I thought I'd be okay."

"But you're not, are you?"

"I'm fine."

He threw a rock into the pool, the rings of water spreading out to the edges where weeping trees bordered the banks. "Your neighbour rang me."

She turned to him, a scowl on her face. "What?"

"Your neighbour, Alex, rang me a few days ago. He said you weren't doing very well and that I should know. He said he knew we were close."

"How dare he! How dare he stick his nose in my business. Is that why you came? You dragged Dad down here when he should probably be at home resting. Wait until I see him."

"Thank God he did ring. Look at you, you're a bloody mess. I've never seen you this bad, even after you broke up with Hugh."

She kicked a rock into the pool. "I think I'm going to sell. It's too isolated and look what's happened. The house is big and I'm not doing great at night by myself here. You have your own life. You might stay for a while but then you'll want to move on. I should go back to the coast."

"Are you kidding me? Do you read the newspapers? There is crime wherever you go. I would say this is usually a quiet country area. People around here probably don't even lock their doors. This was a random event. It will never happen to you again. The best thing is that the mongrel is dead. At least you don't have to worry about him coming back here."

She sat down and dangled her feet in the water. The water was cool and refreshing. Jacob sat down beside her, his bare feet dangling next to hers, the two of them splashing the water into the middle of the pool.

Jacob had always been good at communicating. He had a way of getting her to open up and talk up things she'd been bottling up. She rattled off the entire story, recalling details that she hadn't thought about since that day. "I feel so responsible for Isla going where she shouldn't have and how I went against what they'd normally done with Alex. He protected them so much and I thought he wasn't letting them be adventurous and think for themselves. I wanted them to experience what you and I had. But I should have remembered they weren't my kids. I overstepped the line."

"Is that what Alex thinks?"

"He says I'm being ridiculous, but my gut churns every time I think about how everything came about."

"I had a good talk to him on the phone and he had a lot to say. It seems that you've brought happiness into all their lives and that what you'd done in the short time you've lived here has changed his world and made him remember what's important. He told me he narrowly avoided making one of the biggest mistakes of his life."

She chuckled and threw a rock into the middle of the pool. "Belinda-Maree. She had her claws into him." Turning to Jacob, she couldn't help but grin. "Oh, if only you could have seen her Jacob. Stunning to look at and a figure to die for. You'd know her if you saw her, she's quite well known for her acting roles in one of the soapies."

He gave her a playful shove. "I think I've only ever watched those shows once or twice. Fame and fortune mean nothing to me. You and I, we're the same. Although you nearly got sucked in with Hugh. From my conversation with Alex, it appears that you both have quite a lot in common."

She narrowed her eyes. "What is that supposed to mean?"

"I would say that you mean a bit more to him than just a neighbour or friend."

She sat upright. "Why, what did he say?"

"Not that much. But he didn't need to. I can tell from the way he talks about you how much he cares for you."

She lay back, looking up through the canopy of leaves, the sun filtering through creating dancing dapples across the water. "I thought I had feelings for him too, before everything happened." Shielding her face from the sun, she looked at a kookaburra perched on the branch above them. It tilted its head to the side as if it was listening to their conversation. "Now every time

I'm close to him I feel guilty. Guilty that his daughter was nearly murdered."

"But she wasn't and neither were you. Do you know I thought you were more practical than this? What you're doing is letting an evil person like Lester ruin your life. What do you think Aunt Lucille would say about all of this?"

She sat up as the kookaburra started to laugh, its cackles echoing around the rockpool area. "I know. I know exactly what she would say. I can hear her voice in my head. Thanks for that."

"What's she saying?"

She sighed deeply and sat up, the kookaburra silent again and peering down at her. "She would say, get on with it, Charlie."

Jacob leaned down and splashed some water at her. "That's exactly what I heard her say. "Get on with it, both of you."

Standing up she stretched her arms above her head. "Swim?" she asked.

"Aw come on, sis, you know I hate cold water, plus it's winter."

"It's not that cold today, your clothes will dry out on the walk back."

She pulled on his arm, laughing and encouraging him until both of them slid into the icy water. Diving under she let the water pour over her, its chill waking up every part of her body. She floated on her back, memories of the day she had done similar with Alex, replaying in her mind.

Jacob kicked and swam back and forth, his exaggerated huffing and puffing enough to let her know that the water was more than cold enough for him.

When they hopped out, they stood and watched as another two kookaburras joined the first one on the branch, all three of them cackling loudly.

"We should head back," Charlotte said. "Mum and Dad will be waiting for us."

Linking his arm through hers Jacob led the way back out along the track.

"This area is beautiful. I don't think you should sell. Give yourself time. Let me stay for a while and see how we work together. I give you my word I'll stay for a year and after that if you still want to sell, then okay."

"How are you going to stay for a year? What about your job?"

"I've quit. I need a change and I'm going to have it here, whether you like it or not. Let's give it a go together. I've given it a lot of thought in the last couple of weeks and I'm keen to help you with your business and work together to get the retreat up and running. If you say yes, I'd really like to be a part of it. Not just as a helper or to come and go whenever I feel like it, but rather to take it on as a permanent lifestyle and job. That's why Mum and Dad have come down with me. They wanted to have a good look at the place and see what you thought. Make sure both of us are on the same page. If you agree to me being here permanently, I'll drive them back home after a couple of days and then bring all my stuff back down. What do you say?"

For the first time in many weeks, Charlotte felt like a weight lifted from her shoulders. She'd been trying to take everything on by herself. Usually, she was perfectly capable of doing that, but with everything that had happened, she'd lost some of that bravado and confidence. Now with Jacob here, she could see a clear direction again. He was right. Together it would be easier. They could bounce their ideas off each other and there was still plenty of room to have their own space and life. They should give it a year and see what happened. It would be a joint business.

Chapter 33

Even though the days were warm, at night the chill of winter drifted in and Jacob lit the fireplace so they could sit in the loungeroom. Her father had brought down one of Aunt Lucille's bottles of whiskey and they all enjoyed a glass each on ice, toasting her and Uncle Bernard. For the first time since the morning that Isla had gone missing, Charlotte relaxed. Being with Jacob and her parents reminded her of everything she'd overcome in the previous years and what her intentions and dreams were when she'd purchased Forrest Glen.

Her father loved the property, promising that when he was up to it he'd bring Mum back down and they'd spend some time here. He'd noticed some of the fences needed fixing and he had some plans in his mind for renovating the old shed. "It's a one-in-a-million property, this one. And this old house, it just has a good feel to it. It feels like home."

Her mother sat in the lounge chair, her feet curled up under her, her hair much like Charlotte's, except peppered with greys, wound up in a loose bun on top of her head. "It's as if the paintings were just meant to be here. Like they were always going to hang on these walls. Thank goodness he never stole them. Although, as we always say, they are only material items. Everything can always be replaced. As long as everyone is okay, that's all that matters."

Her parents' practical attitude and the fact that they loved the house and property restored some of her enthusiasm and she talked at length with them and Jacob about her plans for the next couple of months. The idea of selling had taken a back seat and now there was a renewed interest with the idea of Jacob being on board. They were going to sit down and work out finances and a business deal. Although the property was hers, he wanted to ensure that she realised he was serious about being a partner in the retreat business

The next morning she woke with energy and a different mindset. Today was the first day of a new beginning. She'd rung Alex later that morning. "I'd love you and the kids to come over and meet Mum and Dad. Jacob is here too but you'll get a chance to know him anyway because he's going to come and live permanently. He's going to come in on the business with me and ..." She'd stopped talking when he laughed and she realised that she was talking a lot, and fast.

"You reminded me of Isla there for a minute. I'm glad to hear you sounding a bit more like your old self. Yes, of course we'd love to come over."

"We'll have dinner on the verandah so come over about five, and make sure to bring Barney," she added.

She'd set a long table with a white linen tablecloth on it, digging deep into the cupboard to find her best dinner and cutlery sets that had once been Lucille's. Her mother helped her get everything ready while Jacob prepared the meat for the barbeque. "You must miss your sister, Mum," she asked, watching her mother looking fondly at the glasses that Aunt Lucille had always loved.

Her mother pushed her hip up against hers, a playful shove. "I miss her like you wouldn't believe. She was such a bright star in our lives. But my dear, she went how she wanted to and she was never a day in hospital. She loved you and Jacob like you were her own children."

"You know, Mum, when I thought that we were never going to leave that cave, I drew on her and you and Dad for my strength. It was as if Lucille was talking to me, telling me everything would be okay and that I'd see you all again. I'm sure I could hear her voice."

"She would be proud of you and what you've decided to do with her inheritance. You're very much like her in many ways."

"Oh, do you think so? I'd love nothing more than to be like her."

Her dad popped his head in through the window, hearing the last of their conversation. "Just don't drink as much whiskey as she did. I could never keep up with her."

Alex, Barney, and the children arrived right on the dot of five. They'd driven over and Charlotte's heart missed a beat when Alex approached her, bending down to kiss her on the cheek. His hair was ruffled and his eyes sparkled, the dark circles that had been under them the previous week no longer there. A collared shirt and jeans hugged his body and she glanced downwards, loving the leather riding boots he always wore.

"Put my good ones on for the occasion," he quipped, following her eyes.

"Oh, I didn't mean to check out your boots, but I've always admired those and the ones the kids wear." She touched his arm and looked up into his eyes, her smile wide as his eyes looked into hers. It had only been a couple of days since she'd seen him, but she felt like it was weeks. Thank goodness she felt like herself today and the heavy darkness that had hung over the last week had lifted. She turned around as her father coughed loudly, reminding her that there were some introductions to make.

There was lots of banter and laughter as she introduced everyone. They all shook hands and Isla hugged everyone before passing a bunch of flowers to Charlotte's mum. Everyone was dressed up and she thought how lovely Barney looked. He was such a kind man, the perfect gentleman, and her heart melted when he bobbed his head politely when greeting her parents. He shook hands with Jacob and her father, the three of them soon discussing the town of Bindarra and the area around it.

Isla went to check out the treehouse and Eli followed behind her, both of them climbing up on the platform and dangling their legs over the side. They chatted each other, reminding Charlotte of how she and Jacob had once been. Alex appeared behind where she stood in the middle of the yard watching the two of them, shaking her head as they tried to get her to come and join them.

She felt his shoulder next to hers and turned to see him raise his eyebrows in amusement. "Why do those two always think of you like another child. You should hear them talk about you. They forget you're an adult."

"I love that and I need to be reminded to not lose that enjoyment of childish ways. That must be why I wanted to be a teacher. Always surrounded by kids."

His arm brushed against hers as he peered up into the tree. "You sound like you're back to yourself. I've missed your smile," he said.

She linked her arm through his. "I got lost there for a moment. Sometimes I need to be reminded about what's important. I might even forgive you for making a sneaky phone call to my family behind my back."

He laughed as he spoke. "Well, sometimes when people are stubborn, others have to take matters into their own hands." He squeezed her arm, his body close to hers, his words spoken softly. "I think we need to take this discussion up at another time when there aren't so many others around."

She didn't dare turn around, knowing her parents and Jacob would be watching closely. They'd already voiced their suspicions that the good-looking Alex who lived next door might be more than just a friend. Now she was adding fuel to their fire of suspicion. No doubt she'd never hear the end of it once the visitors were gone.

"I'm guessing that my mother is nearly falling off her chair watching us." Charlotte turned to him. "You're right, now is not the time. When is?"

"You said your family are leaving tomorrow. I'll pick you up for dinner. Let's go out. Barney will mind the kids."

His face was close to hers and she looked at his lips and wondered what they would feel like on hers. It was as if he read her mind. "I'd kiss you right here and now, but perhaps we should just start with dinner."

She shook her head as if to get her mind in order, pulling her arm away from his. "What time?"

"Six o'clock. Be ready."

They laughed together before walking back up to the verandah and joining the others. Her mother gave her a quizzical look but she pursed her lips and shook her head. "I'll talk to you later," she whispered as she walked past her into the kitchen. Waves of excitement ran through her body and she rubbed her arm that was tingling where Alex had touched her. Calm down, she told herself. It was just a date. How could a week that had started so badly, transform into a week where everything seemed to be coming together?

Chapter 34

The mood was light as she waved her parents and Jacob off early the next morning. Her father looked healthier and he told her it was from the fresh air and being together as a family.

"Love you, Charlie," he said as he leaned through the car window, grasping her hand and kissing it. "You've made a great choice with this place and I have a feeling your mother and I will be spending some time here in the future."

"I would love that, Dad." She squeezed his hand and blew a kiss to her mother who sat in the back seat of the car.

Jacob leaned across her father. "I'll see you in a couple of days."

"Sounds great. I'll have your bedroom ready for when you come back."

She stood in the driveway until their car was no longer visible. There was plenty to do before Jacob returned. Eventually, he'd have his own cabin but until that was renovated, he'd have to stay in the main house with her. Excitement filled her as she thought of the months ahead. Jacob was as motivated as she was about the opening of the retreat and his ideas had breathed some new inspiration into what was already planned.

Chapter 35

It had been a long time since Charlotte had been so preoccupied with what to wear for a night out. Ridiculous, she thought. Alex had seen her in clothes ranging from old yard clothes to her pyjamas. Attempting to flatten her hair, she pushed it to where she wanted it to sit, but it put up its usual defiance, the curls springing out wildly.

Focus on the outfit, she thought. By the time the decision of what to wear was made, her bed was covered with an array of outfits. A short black dress, the fitted style accentuating her figure, was perfect, and the black stockings hopefully would keep her legs warm. Turning in front of the mirror she adjusted her thick woollen scarf. No doubt the weight she'd lost would come back, particularly when Jacob moved in. Someone else to cook for was exactly what she needed.

Alex arrived on the dot of six and bounded up the back stairs, knocking on the door just as she opened it. He stared hard at her, his eyes looking her up and down. "Wow. You look great. I'm not used to you dressed up."

She turned the key in the door and walked outside with him. "Thank you. It's nice to be going out."

He was the perfect gentleman and opened the car door for her, before getting into the driver's side.

"I've made a booking at the resort a bit out of town. They tell me the food is great. I haven't been there so I hope it lives up to its reputation."

"I've heard good things about it also. Thea from the cafe recommended it." She didn't add how Thea had originally also recommended Alex to her, when she first moved here.

The restaurant was everything they'd heard and more. The food was delicious and the local wine went down smoothly. Alex stopped after his second glass.

"You have another one, I'm going to have a coffee."

The conversation flowed over dinner and she loved discussing what Isla and Eli were up to as well as listening to his plans for the polo season. Now with Lester and other interferences gone, he was keen to have some tournaments on the property. She hadn't questioned what the other interferences were, knowing full well that Belinda had not been in favour of him spending so much time at the farm. Her main aim had been to keep him with her in Sydney. Now he had full range to plan the season the way he wanted. She liked that he hadn't said anything mean about Belinda or even mentioned her name for that matter.

The subject swung to her plans for the retreat. She looked at Alex over the top of her glass, the delicious wine making her face feel flushed. Thank goodness she wasn't driving.

"You'll be pleased," she said. "I've actually taken a booking for next month for cabins one and two. They're not too bad but I'll have to get a move on and spruce them up. They just need a good dust and clean. I have all the new linen and bits and pieces for them, it's just a matter of getting it all in place. Jacob will be back in a couple of days to help."

"That's fantastic. Your adventure is about to start." He raised his coffee cup to her glass and they clinked. "I might need to make some prior bookings for the cabins once I get the polo dates in place. That's if you're interested. They won't be artists or writers but they're going to need accommodation for a couple of nights."

"Of course, I'll take those bookings. First in best dressed."

They were the last to leave the restaurant and stood in the carpark for a long while looking up at the full moon above.

"It's a beautiful night," Alex said, taking her hand as they walked back to the car.

They chatted and laughed all the way home and Charlotte had butterflies in her stomach every time Alex took his eyes off the road and looked her way. When they'd pulled up outside her house she asked if he wanted to come in for a coffee.

"I might get going," he said. "It's not that I don't want to come in, it's just it's getting a bit late and I told Barney I'd be back before midnight. The kids will be asleep, but… you know how it is."

They stood together in her front yard, the moonlight dancing across the paddocks beyond. A horse whinnied from the far paddocks and when she looked up a star fell from high above her.

"Look quickly. Up there." She pointed and Alex took her hand as they looked upwards.

"Make a wish," he said.

As she closed her eyes she squeezed his hand. For a moment she lost sense of time, the warmth of his touch, firm and strong, sending tingling sensations through her body. When she opened her eyes, she looked straight up at him, her body aching with desire as he drew her in, holding her close as his lips pressed down on hers. His body pushed up against her and she reached up to put her arms around his neck. Warm lips closed over hers, his kisses soft and long, his arms firm around her body.

When he finally drew away from her, she took a deep breath. Placing his hands either side of her face he kissed her again and pulled her closer.

Finally, he pulled away. "Goodnight, my beautiful Charlie, and thank you for a fabulous first date."

He waited until she walked up the stairs and unlocked, waving back when she blew him a kiss good-night. As she leaned against the door, she murmured out loud, "And let there be many more."

━━

CHARLOTTE SMILED as she ate her breakfast the next morning. Just as well no one can see me, sitting here grinning by myself, she thought. It had been a long time since she'd felt like this.

Last night had been the start of something new and she wondered how long until she would see Alex again. From the verandah she could see across the paddocks and it looked like another perfect day. The sky was clear and she could feel the winter warmth on her face. Horses in the paddock nearby stood together, soaking up the sun, their tails flicking every so often to chase the flies away. When they put their heads up and looked towards Alex's place she followed their gaze.

When she stood up and looked, her heart thumped hard and she quickly put her plate down, waving her hand high in the air. It was Alex and the kids didn't seem to be with him. He was by himself. He must have seen her wave because he started jogging towards her. Goodness me she hadn't even brushed her hair and this morning she'd thrown on her oldest pair of jeans and a baggy woollen jumper that was way too big for her. She went to meet him but stopped on the top step. The grass was covered in dew and she remembered she'd worn her ugg boots. What a sight!

Alex stopped when he got to the bottom step. As usual, he looked amazing, his blue jeans, leather boots and woollen jumper as if they had just come fresh out of the shop and been tailor-made just for him. This morning a dark stubble covered his cheeks and chin, a soft smile on his face as he greeted her. "Good morning, Charlie. I hope you don't mind me coming over so early, but…" He looked up at her. "How do you manage to look so good no matter what you wear." He stepped up beside her and wrapped his arms around her, the look he gave her sending wild sensations through her body.

They stood staring at each other until finally she managed to speak. "Good morning, Alex. I'm surprised you're alone. How did you manage that?"

He laughed softly, pushing some strands of hair back behind her ears. "I had to be very sneaky. Those two are not silly. They've been asking me all sorts of questions this morning. They know there is something going on." He looked over her shoulder towards his house. "I wouldn't be surprised to see them running across there very shortly."

His hand reached up and stroked her face and she pressed her head into his chest. "Can I just stay like this forever?" she murmured.

Kissing the top of her head, he whispered. "I couldn't wait another second to see you again. I just wanted to hold you to make sure last night was real."

Warm sensations filled her and she didn't want to move. Alex's arms were firm and strong around her and she enjoyed the moment, snuggling into him the best feeling in the world. Eventually he pulled away. "Come and sit for a moment. I want to talk to you properly without Eli and Isla around."

They sat together on the top of the stairs. Both started to speak at the same time and they leaned into each other, Charlotte laughing at the excitement of the moment. In a matter of days her entire world had changed again. Placing her hand on his arm, she began the conversation. "So much has changed so quickly. One minute you were engaged, then you're not and now, well…" she looked up at him. "Now what? Where to from here?"

He cleared his throat and placed his hand on top of hers. "That's what I want to get clear, right from the start." They turned and gazed at each other and he squeezed her hand. "At the moment all I want to do is smother you in kisses and hold you next to me, but…"

"I hate the word, *but*."

"But, we need to talk. I need to know that you feel the same as me and I want to get this, I mean, us, off to the right start."

That's sounds serious," she said, happy for once with what came after the, *but*. "You start. Tell me what you think."

A serious look crossed his face and he looked down at their hands, before turning his eyes back to her face. "I've fallen madly in love with you. A crazy love where all I can think about is you and being near to you. Sleep did not come to me last night and I lay awake until the sun came up." He reached up and stroked her face. "Thinking of you, Charlie, and your kind soul, your beautiful face and the way you are with the kids. As much as I tried not to, I also thought about how I could have lost you..." He held his hand up as she went to speak. "... and Isla and how my fear of something happening to you is the same as for my kids."

When he gripped her hand and pressed his lips against it she took a quick breath in. He waited for an instant before continuing. "If I'm honest with myself I was attracted to you from the first time we met properly, not at the gate that first night but when I really got to talk to you." He took a deep breath. "I love you. I tried not to let it happen but I fell in love with you. Before this, I settled for something, to make someone else happy. I went along with it because I think I'd forgotten what real love was like. Now, well now, I know and I want us to spend time together and let this relationship grow and become something that's special for both of us."

He stopped suddenly. "I've said too much." A worried look crossed his face. "What do you think?"

Reaching up she stroked his face, the stubble rough under her fingers. "She traced his lips with her touch, taking some time before she spoke. "I've fallen in love with you also and I tried not to."

Alex's entire face lit up. "So, we feel the same? This is the start?"

She nodded. "I think about you constantly and thank goodness you came here this morning because I wasn't sure if I should come and see you." She looked across the paddocks, Eli and Isla just visible as they started to make their way towards them. "I don't want to rush into anything though. We've both been through a bit and it will be nice to have our own places and take it slow."

"I feel exactly the same. There's no rush and we can just take each day, week, month as it comes. Years also."

His voice was husky and full of emotion. "We have plenty of time for our relationship, maybe not time for us now though. You have visitors."

They laughed together. "I know you're aware but I will warn you if you take me you take on those two also," Alex quipped, pointing to Eli and Isla who were sprinting through the grass, waving their arms once they spotted Alex and Charlotte.

Wrapping her arm through his she cuddled into his body. "That's one of the best parts. I get three loves for the price of one."

"I know what they'll say."

"What?"

He wrapped his arm around her and pulled her to him. "They'll say what I think. The three of us get you."

As she watched Eli open the gate for Isla, both waiting until Jasper caught up to them, she thought how only a short while ago she had considered leaving. Now a fresh start with Alex beckoned and her heart skipped a beat as he bent down and kissed her.

They both looked up as Isla's loud voice broke the moment. "Oye, you two. We can see you. Ain't nobody got time for that mushy stuff!"

~~~

For your reading pleasure, here is an excerpt from the next book in the Bindarra Creek Mystery Romance series: Protecting their Destiny © Erin Moira O'Hara

CHAPTER **One**

Each step brought Emma closer to her worst nightmare. Cattle yards were her least favourite place in the world. Almost being trampled to death on her twelfth birthday had ensured a fear that didn't look like diminishing anytime soon.

Her heart pounded in her throat as she stepped onto the bottom stock yard rail and reached for the top one, her pregnancy making her movements awkward.

She'd loved hanging around her grandfather's stockyards, absorbing the whistles, dogs barking, cattle bellowing. The sound of hooves thundering as stockman pushed the mob into the yards had been exhilarating. But not anymore. Not since that day. She hadn't been this close to a stock yard in years.

She didn't trust cattle, and she didn't trust Reid's huge stud rams either. Not even Stanthorpe, who had been raised as a pet for the first year of his life. The only animals on Tulachmhor she trusted were the horses and lambs. The horses had ideal temperaments, were easy to handle and obedient. Lambs were cuddly and gorgeous. She didn't mind ewes either, as long as they were out in the paddocks.

From her position on the rail, Emma could see the cattle being herded down the valley towards her. Perspiration dampened her forehead. She gripped the rail tighter.

I can do this. I can't hide away forever. If I'm going to help Reid run Tulachmhor one day, I must overcome this fear.

It would get easier, the Sullivans were gradually

reducing their Hereford numbers as they turned Tulachmhor back into a Merino stud.

Two horsemen at either side kept the cattle from breaking. Another rider brought up the rear, cantering back and forth. From a distance, the mob looked docile. Emma shuddered. Draft the cows from their calves and it would be another matter.

As the riders got closer, she identified Jerry Eckford, the Sullivan's jackaroo. A nice guy she planned to introduce to her best friend. He rode his dapple-grey gelding to the right of the mob. Hunter Sullivan, her soon to be brother-in-law, spurred his bay gelding and blocked a calf's escape on the left.

Her attention shifted to the horseman at the back of the mob. Her fiancé. Two more weeks and he would be her husband. Reid was totally absorbed in moving the mob towards the yards. Sitting relaxed in his saddle, his Akubra shading his face, one hand resting on his thigh, as he whistled up his dog, Gypsy.

Emma took a moment to admire his broad shoulders and easy posture. How she loved this man and his calm way of going about life. His patience and gentle hands as he worked his horse or trained his blue heeler never ceased to impress her. She wouldn't be here now, if it wasn't for a twist of fate and the amazing connection they shared. She could only be grateful for his patience and concentrated effort in pursuing her.

She shivered as the thundering hooves drew closer. If Kathleen hadn't twisted an ankle, she would have been here this morning. After all Reid's grandmother's kindness, it was the least Emma could do to drop off two flasks of coffee and a basket of egg and bacon rolls. If she could just get Reid's attention, she'd hand them over and be on her way to the hospital and her morning clinic.

"Morning, Doctor Fahey. Do ya need a hand climbing over that rail?"

Emma flinched. She hadn't noticed the farmhand in the shadows across the yard. The 43-year-old creep made her uneasy.

"Why on earth would I climb into a yard where a mob of cattle are heading, especially as I'm heavily pregnant?"

He grunted. "Who knows what ya thinking of doin'."

She watched warily as the stocky man sauntered across the yard, his thumbs hooked into the belt under his overhanging stomach, his sleazy gaze fixed on her chest, making her skin crawl. "Shouldn't you be outside the yards, Bob? Don't you need to open the gate?"

"I reckon the boss would rather I kept an eye on you, sweet cheeks."

Emma narrowed her eyes. "Do *not* call me sweet cheeks. It's offensive and bad-mannered. I am perfectly safe here, so please go away."

"Pride goes before a fall, sweet cheeks." He spat on the ground then sauntered away, opening the far gate for the cows and calves streaming down the hillside.

As a child, she'd loved holidays at Hickory Ridge, watching her grandfather and uncle work their stock. Since her near death experience, she preferred to take a quiet ride as far away from the cattle and stockyards as possible.

Her fear of cattle had made no sense to her maternal grandfather. Morgans had been breeding cattle since they settled in Bindarra Creek back in the

1800's. And even though Gramps had been the one to save her life, leaving him with a permanent limp, he'd continued working with cattle until his heart gave out.

Emma looked over her shoulder to the high ridge in the distance, easily seen from all over the district. A Morgan ancestor had planted a row of hickory trees along the top, hence the name Hickory Ridge. The golden acres and rolling hills had been in the Morgan family for generations. It shared a boundary with Tulachmhor, which had belonged to the Sullivans just as long.

She still missed her tough-as-leather grandfather. Before his death, Gramps had often told her he was proud of her achievements but insisted she'd have made an incredible jillaroo. Emma smiled. Apparently, a jillaroo outweighed a gynaecologist any day.

Reid's shout brought her back to earth with a start. She watched in fascination as he leaned forward out of the saddle to chase a calf that had broken away from the mob. Reeling his horse left and right, he headed off the nervous animal.

Emma turned back to the yard and froze. Bellowing cattle, breathing hard, streamed in. She coughed as their hooves churned up the dirt and covered her in dust. Terrifying flashbacks of that awful day bombarded her, locking her fingers to the top rail. She couldn't move.

"Get off the bloody fence, Emma." Reid's shout broke the trance holding her in its grip, enabling her to unlock her fingers. His thunderous scowl sent a shiver down her spine. Within one breath and the next Reid had gone from calm and controlled to aggravated and angry.

She stepped down from the rail, shaking violently as

she desperately tried to stem a different kind of fear. One she hadn't had to face since leaving Sydney. A fear she refused to face ever again.

Her eyes widened as an agitated cow charged the fence. It veered away at the last moment but left Emma's heart pounding in her chest. The cow forced her way through the entering herd and out of the yards again. Emma watched as Reid wheeled his horse to chase the runaway, shouldering it to turn the beast back. The runaway kicked up her heels then followed the last of the cattle into the stockyard.

Hunter rode forward and shut the gate. He was as tall and broad as Reid, and they shared the same brown hair and green eyes. From all accounts, he'd mellowed since marrying Emma's cousin. Yet right now, he looked savage. They both did and it scared her much more than a herd of cattle ever would.

"You okay, Doc?"

Emma dragged her eyes from her fiancé and his brother to Jerry Eckford, as he drew his snorting gelding up outside the fence. She nodded. "I'm fine." Her gaze flicked to Bob Farrell, smirking at her from the other side of the yard. "I do not like that man. He's rude and obnoxious."

"I agree, Doc. Reid wouldn't have hired him if we weren't shorthanded. He won't last long, take my word for it. Best you stand well back. With a herd this size, they can be unpredictable."

"I know. I just froze for a moment."

Jerry removed his hat and wiped his shirt sleeve across his sweaty forehead. He had a rugged complexion and gentle hazel eyes. "I reckon you've given Reid a few white hairs today. He almost fell off

Zeus when he saw you at the rail. I've never seen you at the cattle yards."

"Kathleen asked me to bring down breakfast, but I see you've still got a lot to do."

"Yeah. Today, we're drafting the cows from their calves. Deciding which heifers to retain as breeders and get the culls into the forcing pens before the trucks arrive."

Reid cantered up and dismounted. He was covered in dust. "What the hell are you doing here, Emma?"

Jerry frowned at Reid before spurring his horse and trotting away.

"I brought breakfast." Emma turned on her heel and stalked over to a tree stump table and chair setting where she'd left the basket of egg rolls and coffee flasks.

Reid followed, leading Zeus behind him. "Emma, I appreciate the thought, but we had breakfast hours ago."

"It wasn't my idea." She picked up the cane basket. "Here." She shoved it into Reid's chest. "Your grandmother twisted her ankle this morning. She's fine but needs to rest it. There's coffee too. I've done my good deed for the day. See you later."

"Emma, wait." Reid dropped Zeus' reins and placed the basket back on the table. "I'm sorry I yelled at you. I wasn't expecting to see you at the yards. You scared me."

"The fences are solid, and I wasn't in any danger of falling into the yards."

"Yeah, but you're carrying a wide load and not as quick on your feet as usual."

"I beg your pardon?" She wacked his shoulder. "A *wide* load?"

He grimaced. "Baby. You're carrying a baby. Thanks for bringing us a second breakfast. We have worked up an appetite and coming to the stockyards took guts. I'm proud of you, Em."

"I'm proud of me too." Maybe she'd overreacted. "I didn't mean to scare you, and I'm sorry if it caused friction between you and Hunter."

"Don't worry about it. We're always having a go at each other." He walked with her to the driver's side of her Beetle, opened the door then kissed her. "Enjoy your last day at work."

"I plan to. What's on your agenda today?"

He sighed. "Once we get these vealers loaded, I've got to see why one of our windmills is not pumping."

"Okay, don't overdo it." She climbed into her Beetle. "I'll see you after work."

"You will." He winked. "Every inch of me, if you want."

"Don't be naughty." Emma grinned as he closed the door then she took her time putting on her seat belt and starting the engine. She watched her soon-to-be husband call the other men over for breakfast. Apparently, they were going to eat before separating the cattle.

She exhaled and released the brake. She'd done it. Stood beside a stockyard crammed with cattle. It had taken every ounce of courage she possessed, but she'd done it. She'd overcome one of her biggest fears. Cattle weren't so bad, as long as she wasn't in the yards with them. In two weeks, she'd overcome her another fear. She'd marry the man of her dreams. She wouldn't be running away from this man a week before the wedding.

Reid watched the woman he loved drive away in her

yellow Volkswagen Beetle. He really was proud of Emma, even though she'd scared him. She'd taken a big step today, coming down to the stockyard despite her crippling fear of the cattle.

He unpacked the basket, his thoughts still on Emma. It had been an almighty battle convincing her to move in with him two years ago. Her terror of cattle and cattle yards had only been one hurdle. He hadn't expected to fall in love with a woman who shared his aversion to marriage and children. It hadn't mattered at first, but as time went on, he wanted what his brother and sisters had. And he wanted everyone to know Emma was his.

Getting Emma to choose a date had been his biggest hurdle. Her pregnancy hadn't swayed her an inch, and he couldn't figure out why.

He'd had a violent and neglectful mother who'd ruined his childhood. She was responsible for creating the trust issues he carried with him even now, but Emma came from a stable, loving home. He couldn't help but think that there was more to her aversion to marriage. Something deep that she wasn't ready to share with him yet.

Leaving Zeus to graze on clumps of grass, Reid set out four mugs on the roughly hewn table they sat around most mornings. He poured coffee into each then sat on tree stump to eat his egg and bacon roll.

Hunter sat on the stump next to him. "Got something on your mind, Reid?"

He took a mouthful of sweetened coffee, savouring the taste as he met his brother's questioning look. "I was just thinking about our feud with the Morgans."

Hunter chuckled. "The ancestors would be turning in their graves."

"What feud?" Bob Farrell claimed a stump opposite, glancing between Hunter to Reid. "I thought you fellas got on well with Jake and Riley Morgan."

"They do now," chimed in Jerry with a laugh. "Not that long ago these two took every opportunity to outwit, outride, and outthink Riley and Jake Morgan. It's been that way between both families for generations."

"Why?" Bob's confusion had Reid grinning.

"I hear way back in the day, one stole the other's fiancée, and they fought over who owned an allotment of land fronting the river. The feud grew and lasted until six years ago."

"What happened six years ago," asked Bob.

Jerry chuckled. A pretty, green-eyed lady arrived in town. She was searching for her biological mother and ended up bringing the Sullivans and Morgans together. Now these guys are all best mates."

"The right woman will do that to a man." Hunter raised an eyebrow at Reid. "Isn't that right, bro?"

"You should know, Hunter. You fell the hardest."

"Look who's calling the kettle black." Hunter held up his cup. "To the women we love. May they always welcome us home with open arms and warm hearts."

Reid shook his head. "You've gone soft in your old age, mate."

"Nope. It's called domestic bliss." Hunter's lips twitched. "Except when the terror twins are teething. That's called sleep deprivation."

Reid laughed. In five weeks, he'd have his own son or daughter to cherish and keep safe. The thought terrified him. If his own father hadn't known his children were suffering, how would he?

. . .

A BINDARRA CREEK Mystery Romance series – released from July 2022

Amulet of Death – Suzanne Gilchrist (aka S E Gilchrist)

Beyond the Gate – Rhonda Forrest

Protecting their Destiny – Erin Moira O'Hara

Only She Knew – Linda Charles

Secrets of River Cottage – Annie Seaton

Forgotten Secrets – Susanne Bellamy

A Perfect Danger – Phillipa Nefri Clark

ABOUT THE BINDARRA CREEK SERIES

WELCOME TO BINDARRA CREEK, a struggling country town where people work hard and love deeply. Set in the picturesque tablelands of New England, Australia, Bindarra Creek is a fictional, rural community full of romance, intrigue, adventure, drama and suspense.

To date there are four multi-author 'series' set in the Bindarra Creek world all written by best-selling Australian romance authors. A fifth is planned for late 2022 – **A Bindarra Creek Christmas.**

FULL DETAILS on buy links for all books in Bindarra Creek world can be found at:

www.bindarracreekromance.com

About the Author

Rhonda Forrest is an Australian author who juggles writing and publishing, along-side teaching high school students. She writes captivating contemporary and historical/romance fiction about relationships, family life and social issues, set amidst beautiful and uniquely Australian landscapes.

After bringing up three daughters and traversing several careers, Rhonda went on to teach creative writing, English and history. Her passion for literacy, history and travelling around Australia fuels her novels. Along with her husband, she divides her time between Tamborine Mountain and a century-old cottage with a rambling garden overlooking the waters of the Whitsundays.

Recent novels bring to life the remarkable characters and settings that make up the unique Australian heritage and take the reader on a journey from bush to beach, with steamy romances, riveting history and eclectic characters.

Some books are available in audio and large print and you can also find some titles available in Portuguese, Publisher- Leabhar Books Brazil.

If you enjoyed this book or any of Rhonda's other books, you can make a big difference by writing a review, or leaving a star rating on Amazon, Goodreads or Bookbub. A personal recommendation to family, friends, libraries and book clubs is another great way to share the books with others. You can also follow Rhonda on Facebook, Instagram, Goodreads and Bookbub.

Author's favourite - sample chapters from *Silkworm Secrets* are in the back of this book.

Website - https://www.rhondaforrest.com/

WE'LL MEET AGAIN SERIES

by Rhonda Forrest

BOOK 1 - *'A dingo howls, a star falls.*
Don't worry for me, I'll be home soon.'

Based on actual events, *Elizabeth's Star* begins the story of Michael and Joanie, unfolding the lives of their families and friends while following the life of Gracie, a little girl left behind when her father went to war.

A moving tale of love, loss, and separation.

BOOK 2 - *'When you go home, tell them of us and say, for your tomorrow, we gave our today.' John Maxwell Edmonds 1918*

Until We Meet is an epic war saga based on actual events that continues the story of Elizabeth's Star. A tale of survival, love and family, set amidst the backdrop of World War II.

BOOK 3 - *My troubles are all over, and I am at home; and often before I am quite awake, I fancy I am still in the orchard at Birtwick, standing with my friends under the apple trees.' (Black Beauty)*

We'll Meet Again is a story of devotion and family, a connection between those who suffered loss and separation and a sweeping tale of hope, chance and love.

SILKWORM SECRETS - Dark Secrets from a Distant Past

(For your enjoyment - Sample chapters at the back of this book.)

'The ancient trees with their rough bark wrap around me like silk cocoons. Their solid trunks and tendril roots grip the ground as if to say, I will hold you, I will not let go.'

SILKWORM SECRETS - Silkworm Secrets Series Book 1

In the 1960s the rural suburbs of Brisbane should have been an idyllic place for Ruby and Bobby to grow up. Their treehouse retreat, set high in a mulberry tree is a place to share friendship and watch the events of the yards nearby. However as the two become teenagers, the naive Ruby is exposed to the sinister events that Bobby has to deal with in his family life. As the years pass and the best friends go their separate ways, childhood events become a distant memory. Will the dark secrets remain uncovered or will Ruby and Bobby be forced to face up to what they witnessed so many years before.

This is a story about the secrets that children keep, the strength that comes from a childhood friendship and a special family love that overcomes the hardships of the past.

***

Mary – reviewer Goodreads - *Yes it's true this novel explores deeper and darker issues, - but life can be like that, complex, difficult, unfair. A rollercoaster ride of emotion but well worth it. This quintessential Australian novel is a must-read.*

October 2022 - FOREVER MORE

The days pass for Ruby and Bobby just how they like: slow and peaceful with plenty of time for the two of them. The dark secrets they once shared have faded into the past, and their life in the Sunshine Coast Hinterland is full of activity as they build their new business. A few head of cattle, a couple of horses, and their dog Rusty complete their family. It's hard to imagine that anyone could want anything more.

However, when family connections from long ago surface, Ruby and Bobby face responsibilities they hadn't anticipated. Bobby is reminded of his own tumultuous upbringing and the two of them make decisions that will change the paths of everyone involved.

Forever More, continues the story of Bobby and Ruby and reminds us of the good and bad in people and that, a loving family can come in many different forms.

TWO HEARTBEATS

When Jess heads west for a fresh start in a small mining town, the dusty, outback plains are a far cry from her former life in the city. Despite having no knowledge of country life, she finds herself loving the isolation and local people who she lives with. All she has to do is keep her head down and work hard to create a better life for herself and Johnno, the only person she has ever truly cared about.

Happy Valley BooksRead —

Amazing authentic relatable characters, the harsh but beautiful Australian country settings and a storyline of realness that you can connect to. This wonderful Australian writer knows how to pull her reader into the plot and bring all the feelings bubbling to the top!

Brenda - Goodreads' Reviewer - *Two Heartbeats' by Aussie author Rhonda Forrest is a story of second chances; of hope; sadness; love and trust. Set in the vast and drought-ridden Australian outback with nothing but dust, flies and heat for company, Two Heartbeats is another emotional novel from an author I thoroughly enjoy.*

Also available as an audio book - Two Heartbeats Audible

TIME WILL TELL - Sequel to *TWO HEARTBEATS*

A rural love story, where friendship, romance and hearts entwine.

When Jess discovered love with Daniel in the tiny outback town of Gowrie, her previous troubled life was cast aside. However, differences in their backgrounds, her doubts about real love and the urge to return and support her twin brother Johnno, forced her to make a decision to leave.

A new home in the small community of Tamborine Mountain provides an opportunity to contemplate how she really feels and what is important. Johnno lives nearby and new friends and a romantic encounter give her a fresh start, but is this what she really wants? And if it isn't, will Daniel welcome her back with open arms?

The tranquil setting of Tamborine Mountain joins forces with the outback of Queensland to continue the story of *Two Heartbeats*. Will the decision be taken out of Jess's hands, pushing her further away, or will her heart lead her to where she will find true happiness?

The Mad Hatter – Book Reviews

When I read Rhonda's work, I think "authentic". There is no pretense. Just raw, honest and beautifully crafted characters and dialogue.

Rhonda writes with such emotion and compassion that it oozes from the pages, very raw and honest. Happy Valley Books Read

KICK THE DUST

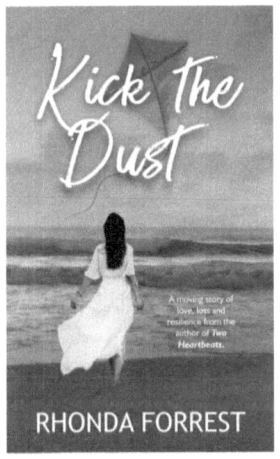

'If I close my eyes, it's easier to hold onto a memory. When I open them, I think it might really be there in front of me.'

After three tours of duty in Afghanistan, Liam Andrews is home safe in Queensland. His weekly life drawing class, full of colourful local artists, helps him manage his post-traumatic stress disorder. But he's struggling to open up about a past that still haunts him.

Belourine 'Billy' is an Afghan refugee who lost everything before arriving in Australia as a child. She finds joy in her daily swims in the lake. After years of upheaval, she's still searching for a place to call home. But her past makes it hard to trust people.When Liam and Billy meet, they form an instant connection. But will they ever overcome the past? And will it be together?

***

Praise for Kick the Dust -

Telma Rocha - *Canadian Author* - *Rhonda Forrest's books always captivate and touch my heart, and this one did too, just as much as all her other books. Her story telling style is unique, full of emotion, and her characters come to life instantly. This book deals with themes of: war, refugees, immigration, PTSD, friendship, and art.*

The Shack by the Bay

An isolated fishing shack on a beautiful bay in the Whitsundays provides Luke with a retreat where he can find peace and solitude. However, the discovery of family war relics, and a developing relationship with the beautiful Lily, connects family histories and reveals a story that threatens to destroy his chance at real happiness.

Will the wartime secrets prove to be the breaking point for a beautiful romance? Or can two families put the deeds of the past behind them?

Romantic and purely Australian, The Shack by the Bay captures the pristine beauty of the Whitsundays and the wartime memories of older Australians while introducing an eclectic blend of friends and family.

***

Review comments - *An intriguing mix of historical romance, a coming of age, love and its complications against the backdrop of World War II.*

Praise for The Shack by the Bay - *A novel that offers a linkage between the present and past while showcasing the natural beauty of a spectacular slice of Australia.*

'The ancient trees with their rough bark wrap around me like silk cocoons. Their solid trunks and tendril roots grip the ground as if to say, I will hold you, I will not let go.'

CHAPTER 1

There had been great excitement the day the silk-worms first came to the treehouse. Walking knee-deep through the dense covering of ferns and bushes beneath the mulberry tree, Bobby had announced that he had a surprise for Ruby in his satchel. It was dim and cool under the tree, the knotted branches and canopy forming a shady, secluded area, only a few frilly-necked lizards and the occasional brown snake sharing the space with the two of them.

She had tried to get him to stop and open his bag, the suspense almost too much, but he kept walking, determined for once not to let her win.

'Wait, Ruby Rose. Just wait until we climb up and then I'll show you.'

'But what is it? Can't you tell me? I'll die of curiosity.'

Ruby liked to be in charge and know everything. The suspense made her climb erratically, stopping and starting,

continually looking down at Bobby climbing steadily below her.

'Just get up there and I'll show you,' he said.

Standing on her toes, she balanced on the rungs leading up the tree. He noticed the bottoms of her feet, dark purple colours mixed with dirt from the earth below. Her flowery cotton dress was also stained purple from where she had sat on some of the thousands, perhaps millions, of berries that had dropped from the tree during the fruiting season.

Above them, the trail of timber blocks, like steps, wove their way up into the darkest reaches of the tree. Nails that had long ago been hammered into the rough, textured bark held the timber secure, and as they climbed higher, tiny glimpses of the sky became visible; a blue backdrop to the thick branches that reached upwards, their tops covered by the dense canopy of weeping smaller branches and leaves.

Perched amongst the thick foliage of the massive mulberry tree the treehouse was obscured, a safe haven, a place no one else bothered with, tucked away in an overgrown corner of Ruby's backyard. The two best friends considered the spot to be the best place in the world, and its location among other large trees—figs, mangoes and a towering pine tree—provided them with their own secret corner, a safe house with no adults, just the two of them, talking, laughing; conspirators.

'Hurry up.' Ruby used her bossy voice as she held up the canvas for Bobby to enter the treehouse.

Once inside he had reached into his satchel and presented Ruby with a number of pieces of cardboard, all covered in multitudes of silkworm eggs. She was ecstatic and caused him great embarrassment by continually hugging him and then jumping up and down, making the treehouse creak and shake a little.

It had been school holidays and they had watched every day, Ruby recording in her notebook when the tiny, grey eggs stuck to the cardboard had lightened in colour.

Finally the day they had both waited so patiently for: tiny silkworms, hundreds of them, wriggling, squirming and climbing over each other, filling an old school port, safe in their new home.

Although Ruby had only been eight, she was fastidious about keeping records of events that occurred in and around the mulberry tree. She left her small notebook in the treehouse, only removing it when she needed to record major incidents. Today she wrote: *143 healthy silkworms. All eating leaves.*

The silkworms grew quickly, fattening on the never-ending supply of leaves from the mulberry tree that seemed to be at its best, the thick canopy dripping with the heaviness of its foliage and fruit. The job of picking the greenest leaves from the tree and making sure that all the worms were fed had been allotted to Bobby. Bobby's other job was to clean the droppings from the boxes so the silkworms would have enough room to move around.

They had found extra boxes, the original school port now overflowing with fat silkworms that quickly ate through the leaves. Their droppings were bright green, an indication, Ruby told Bobby, that they were happy and healthy.

Once, when Ruby was not around, Bobby had carried the largest container, the school port, down the tree and into his bedroom at home. Plugging in the vacuum cleaner, he had tried—just using the pointy end of the vacuum and not the brush part as he later explained to Ruby—to suck up the droppings and give the container a really good clean.

Ruby had not been impressed and had efficiently recorded in her notebook:

September 24, 1968, 54 large fat silkworms. Now only 12 surviveing.

Bobby and vacum encident.

NOW SHE NEEDED to make more notes regarding the latest incident. Bobby stood beside her as she recorded in her neat handwriting:

March 4, The accident, 1970.

School port moths, 17 healthy moths, now only 7 surviveing, 2 of those are injared becous of falling from tree.
Bobby and Ruby falling over encident acident.

' WHAT?' Ruby said as she looked up at Bobby, his mouth opening as if to speak.

Perhaps it 's not the best time to point out her spelling mistakes, he thought, as he closed his mouth, instead smiling and shaking his head. ' You're the best club president,' he said, 'and at least we still have some moths, even after the accident yesterday.'

The small girl rolled her eyes at him, an indication that she was not impressed with the situation.

He had long ago decided to ignore Ruby's habit of eye rolling, as well as to go along with most of the ideas she came up with. The time he spent with her was his only sliver of happiness in amongst the misery of home and school, and he would do anything to keep the peace between them, whatever it took to stretch out the time before he had to return home. Even though the happenings of the day before had been calamitous to Ruby, they hadn't even rated in his own list of personal disasters.

Ruby was oblivious to the situation at his house. Although he sometimes longed to tell her what was really happening, he had decided that for now it was better to keep it that way, to keep it all to himself. Just try not to think about it, he told himself.

CHAPTER 2

THE ACCIDENT HAD HAPPENED the day before, on what had started out as a typical afternoon but had quickly gone wrong; a disastrous chain of events resulting in their moth tally decreasing to just seven.

As usual, they had both rushed home after school and made their way up into the treehouse as quickly as possible. They lay side by side, enjoying the cool of the rough timber flooring in their meeting area.

Bobby was happy to lie still and listen to Ruby as she chattered on about making a new area that she wanted to call the sitting area. Although there were many sections to the treehouse, designated and specified, it was, after all, not such a big structure. They had drawn boundary lines for the different areas on the floor with white chalk, the faint lines invisible in places where their bare feet or bodies had rubbed over them.

Now they sprawled out with their heads in the spying area, feet pushed up against the stump of the activity table, their bodies stretched across three areas— spying, meeting and activities.

Bobby, being the elder and taller of the two, lay contorted, with his knees bent high and his neck twisted slightly so he could fit across the largest flat area of the treehouse. He tried to stretch out his long legs, sinewy from years of school sport and running, before resigning himself to the cramped conditions. Turning his head, he looked through the slits in the timber walls. His intense brown eyes were set deeply, and his tousled dark hair, springy with the Queensland summer humidity, framed his squarish, still boyish face.

Ruby was stretched out fully beside him with her shoulder jammed up against his, her bare feet nowhere near the stump-table that hindered the comfort of the taller Bobby. Conspirators; two sets of eyes flickering back and forth, lying deathly still as if their lives depended on invisibility.

'I told you it was a good idea,' Ruby whispered, indicating the rolled-down canvas across the doorway. ' There's no way anyone can see in now.'

'You're smart for a girl. Sometimes.'

Bobby's chuckle was cut short by the cutting look, a savage glare as the small girl turned towards him, glinting green eyes scowling, her scrunched-up face willing him to remain silent. They stared hard at each other and Bobby concentrated on her face as he counted the biggest freckles, a smattering of cute brown spots across her nose that faded into each other as they ran across the top of her somewhat chubby cheeks. There were a couple of gaps in her teeth where adult incisors had failed to come through quickly enough to mask the fact that she was still young enough to be losing baby teeth.

Knowing better than to tease Ruby about still having teeth like a baby, he kept his quick words to himself rather than incur the wrath and sharp retorts that would flow forth from her; so young but already more than capable of sticking up for herself.

Wavy blonde hair spread out beneath her, so long that it reached below her red cotton shorts. Her thin brown legs were stretched out beside him as she tried to match the length of his own. Ruby didn't like to be far behind Bobby in anything, and she was always measuring her height, telling him that one day they would be the same size.

'But you'll never be as strong as me,' he would say, flexing his muscles, thinking that one day he would have muscles as strong as Popeye in the cartoon pictures.

'My dad says that I can do anything a boy can do,' Ruby said. 'Just because I'm a girl doesn't mean I can't do stuff. He reckons I can do whatever I want, and if I want to be the strongest person, well, I can be.'

'Girls can't do some things that boys can.' Bobby looked at her, suspicious of her confidence and confused about her ideas, so different from what was promoted in his house.

'Of course they can. I can be whatever I want. If I want to be a doctor, well, I can.'

'That's not right. Girls should be nurses or mums.'

'My dad says if I want to be an astronaut like Neil Armstrong then I can be. He says I'm really smart, and when I grow up I can be whatever I want.'

'Bet you can't be a concreter like him.' 'Bet I could.'

'Girls are supposed to get married and have babies. They look after the kids and cook, clean the house.'

'I don't like cooking and cleaning. I hate cleaning the bathtub. I'm going to do something else when I'm grown up.'

'Like what?'

'I'm going to be a lawyer.'

' You mean like on *Homicide*?' he said, referring to the popular television show.

'Yeah, you know, they solve crimes.'

'I thought you weren't allowed to watch those shows. How do you know what a lawyer is when you aren't allowed to watch it?'

'Silkworm secret,' Ruby said. 'If I lie in bed with the door open, I can see the TV screen reflected in the big mirror on the sideboard. My dad's a bit deaf so he has it up pretty loud. I get to see most TV programs, but you can't tell him or Mum.'

'Lawyers are always men.' 'I watch *Matlock Police* too.'

'Your dad would be really angry if he knew you were watching those programs. You'll get in trouble if you get caught.' 'Bobby, I won't get caught. Besides, they're really scary, so most of the time I put my hands over my eyes.'

'You're so lucky that your mum and dad care about you. I wish my parents were like yours. The other day Theresa asked me how you get a new mum and dad. She's tired of all the trouble at home and the way Sally doesn't get looked after properly. I didn't know what to say. I wish I was older, then I'd run away and take them both with me.'

The two best friends stared hard at each other as they talked. It was a game they often played: who could go the longest without blinking. Both blinked sharply, however, when a loud voice bellowed up from under the tree.

'Ruby, you climb down here this minute. I know you're up there. I wasn't born yesterday.' Footsteps scuffed through the thick layer of fallen leaves, moving closer, the voice booming out again. 'You get down here *now*. I've got jobs for you to do and you're not supposed to play until your homework's done.'

The two conspirators, who had no intention of moving or answering, pulled faces at each other, imitating the adult face below.

'Your father will clip you across the ears when you come down and there' ll be no ice cream for you tonight.' Mary, Ruby's mum, waited for a reply. ' You're wasting my time, Ruby. I've got better things to do than look for you. I'm telling you now, though, if you didn't change and you've got mulberry on that school uniform there'll be hell to pay.'

The exasperated voice faded away as Ruby's mum made her way back to the house.

'She's not really mad,' Ruby whispered. 'She just likes to sound like she is, making out she's the boss.'

Bobby looked worried. 'Are you sure your dad won't thrash you?'

The small girl's laughter resounded off the rough timber walls. 'Are you joking? My dad loves me too much. He would never hit me.'

'Does your mum ever hit you?' Bobby was trying to manoeuvre his neck, which was starting to feel like it would be attached sideways on his body permanently.

Ruby's little face scrunched up, her eyes narrowing.'She loses it sometimes, especially when I keep going on about something. Because I'm more stubborn than her, she knows she can't beat me. I can always tell when she's really mad because her face goes red and her eyes … it's like she's a dragon and there's flames coming out of them, red flames licking out of her green eyes. And sometimes her lips go real thin and mean, like this.' Ruby sat up and gave a demonstration.

' What does she do? Does she use a belt?' ' Worse than that.'

'A cricket bat? A broom handle?' 'Don't be silly.'

'I know,' Bobby said, 'the whippy wire out of the curtains.' His curiosity was aroused as he imaged the horrendous punishment her mother might inflict.

' Way worse.' Ruby loved having Bobby's full attention. 'She goes all quiet, then she starts whispering all the angry things she wants to say to me.'

'You mean she doesn't scream or yell?'

Ruby rolled her eyes. 'No, she goes quieter and quieter, telling me off, saying she's going to tell Dad all the bad things I do.'

'Then what?'

'She snaps off a branch, a thin little branch from the wattle tree out the front. She sort of tests it in the air and then real quick, before I can run away, she twitches me with it.'

'Across your face?'

'No, stupid, across the back of my legs, and it stings like crazy and sometimes it leaves a red mark. If I rub it really hard I can make it stay there until Dad gets home and then I tell him that she whipped me with a thick tree branch.'

'Is that it? A bit of a whack from a wattle twig across your legs?'

' Well, it stings.'

'That's nothing, a little wattle twitch.'

'If I put it on real good and make out it hurts a lot,' Ruby said, 'when I sit with Dad at night he rubs it for me. Then he sort of lectures me, tells me how to get around Mum, how not to annoy her. You know the sort of stuff: "Your mother loves you, you need to be nice to her, don't bite the hand that feeds you." Dad reckons she's the boss.'

Bobby lay without speaking, staring up at the patchy tin roof. 'Bobby, are you listening to me? Do you reckon your mum's the boss?'

A lengthy silence followed before he spoke. ' There's

no way Mum's the boss. You know my old man; you've seen what he's like. He's not kind like your dad.'

'Your dad's always nice to me,' Ruby said, 'and he gives me a little sausage when we go to your meat shop, and sometimes he makes Mum laugh. He always chats to her, tells her she has a pretty dress on, says he can smell her dinners cooking and that she must be the best cook in the street.'

'Ha.'

'Mum says that your dad has done really good to have such a big shop, and Dad reckons your dad is a good butcher giving us the meat cheaper, and he says that your sister Theresa works hard, she does really good at school, and Mum and Dad think you're smart, and your Uncle Mike, well, Mum says, "Fancy having an uncle that knows the prime minister, real high up in the government he is, and he has so much money and—"'

Bobby cut her off, wondering how she could speak for so long without a breath. 'You know things aren't always what they seem to be.'

'Like how?'

'Just … never mind.' He stretched out his stiffening muscles. 'What do you mean? Don't start something and not finish it.' 'I mean sometimes things look good to other people, but

they're only seeing what's on the outside.' ' Well, what's on the inside?'

'Forget it. I'm going to get your stupid records book so you can write up the tally.' Bobby sat up suddenly, signalling an end to the conversation.

'Hey, I'm the boss.' Ruby grabbed Bobby as he tried to stand up, his long legs wobbly and unsteady after lying cramped and still for so long. 'Just because you're older—'

And that was when, in a split second, it happened: 'the accident' as Ruby liked to refer to it.

It was like watching a slow-motion movie. Ruby gasped out loud as Bobby's legs became tangled, his body twisted, and he lurched unsteadily towards the table in the centre of the treehouse. The piece of fibro that made up the top of the table rested on the stump of a huge branch. Apart from the way the tabletop crumbled a little around the edges from time to time, it made a perfect flat surface for many of their activities.

That day a number of containers were lined up neatly across the table: an old school port with broken hinges, its stickers peeling; two shirt boxes, the colours on their sides faded and blurry; and two smaller shoeboxes. All the lids on the containers had been punched with multiple holes, providing air for the tiny creatures within.

Ruby's eyes widened as Bobby stumbled and fell forward, one arm reaching out to steady himself and stop his face smashing into the boxes on the table. His hand made contact and he grasped wildly at the closest object. Before their eyes, the largest container, the school port, turned over, the lid going one way, and the rest of the port flipping forward and landing upside down in the reading area.

'Shit.' Bobby gathered himself, standing steady, looking from Ruby to the school port.

They both knew. They knew that below that port, which was now lying lidless in the centre of the reading area, were gaps in the timber floor that opened to the ground far below. This was serious. Bobby registered the fact that Ruby hadn't reprimanded him for swearing; rule number five on the list of Silkworm Club rules.

Ruby crawled slowly over to the port and waited for Bobby. Together they lifted it, cautiously moving it straight up and not sliding it, or allowing it to have any more contact with the floor than necessary.

'Uh-oh.'Bobby pursed his lips and waited for Ruby's response. 'They've nearly all fallen through the gaps,' Ruby said. 'They won't live, they can't fly.' Her voice was shaky as she carefully tried to pick up the contents that had fallen from the container. Bobby pressed his face to the openings between the floorboards, one eye closed, trying to spy any survivors of the fall. Ruby's voice took on the steadiness and authority of the Silk-worm Club president. 'I'll pick these ones up. Can you please go down and see if you can find any on the ground?'

She scooped up the mulberry leaves scattered on the floor, a few silkworm moths gripping to their surface, their delicate wings flapping wildly, their eyebrows furrowed. 'It looks like there are about five here. That means twelve are missing. This morning there were seventeen.Hurry up, Bobby, they only live for a few days so we need to find them and put them back in the box. Then they can lay their eggs.'

As usual, Bobby followed her instructions. Even though he was older by three years, Ruby was the club president, and besides, she was good at organising every-thing and everybody. It was easier to just follow her directions and do what he was told.

He scrambled down the tree trunk, hanging onto the timber steps and hand guides that wound their way down to the ground. The thought of looking for white moths that had probably drifted off on the wind made him smile. He knew that the heavy leaf litter and dense ferns growing wild under the tree would envelop and hide a free-falling silkworm moth that had no sense of surviving in the wild.

But he would try; he would do anything to please Ruby because she was, after all, his best friend.

CHAPTER 3

Dad says you've just got to get on with stuff,' Ruby said as she tidied the treehouse. 'Step forward and don't cry over spilt milk. I' ll bring a mat up and put it over the gaps in the floor.'

The boxes on the table were now lined up straight. Everything had to be in its place and she cast her eyes over the timber boxes, squinted and then rolled her eyes when she noticed the ice-cream tin with a few large mouldy mulberries left in it. 'Got it.' Bobby tipped the few remaining mulberries out the window, replacing the container in its correct position on the shelf. Amused at how neat she had to have everything, he watched her move the crate chairs so they were even and straight.

They both ran their hands over the boxes that were full of cocoons. When the moths hatched, they would hopefully add to their now decreased tally.

'See you in the morning,' Ruby said to the silkworms.

Bobby held up the canvas for her as they made their way out of the treehouse and into the real world below.

When they reached the bottom of the tree they sat for a while, balancing on the huge protruding roots that were covered in the same rough bark as the trunk;

sections of the roots smooth however, due to the continuous movement of bare feet across them over the years.

'I have to go in,' Ruby said eventually. 'It's nearly night.

Even Dad will go mad if I come in after dark.'

'I better go home, too. I still have to do all my jobs before Dad gets home. I'm sorry about the moths, Ruby Rose.'

'Best friends don't get mad with each other. It was sort of my fault, too.'

Emerging from the cover of the trees, they turned in the direction of their houses, both looking up at the horizon as the fading light threw an orange hue over the backyard. Ruby saw the light flick on over the back veranda and knew her dad would be starting to look at the clock, wondering if he should call her in to clean up before dinner.

'See you tomorrow.' Bobby sounded despondent, sad.

He never wants to go home, Ruby thought. He must really like the silkworms, and me, better than his own family.

The darkening light separated them, the clicking of the side gate indicating that Bobby was in his own yard.

Sure enough, Ruby's dad Francis was sitting out on the back steps, his work boots and socks kicked off to the side as he enjoyed a smoke in the balmy evening light. She ran towards him, her small legs going, as her dad would say at a million miles an hour. Placing his cigarette down on the brick stairs beside him, he held both arms out as she jumped onto him. Chubby arms wrapped around his neck, her kisses smothering his face.

'My Ruby Rose, my little mulberry fairy,' he said,

squeezing her tightly, his face nuzzling into her blonde wavy hair.

'I'm never going to let go of you.' Ruby clung to him, her mulberry-stained face squashed into the hairs on his chest, her legs drawn up so she could nestle in, snug and secure.

' What have you been up to today, little one?' He moved her to one side so he could puff on his cigarette.

'Dad, Dad, you'll never believe what happ—'

Her mum's voice interrupted them. 'Right, you two, the pair of you, grubs. One covered in mulberry, the other in concrete dust. You need to clean up before you come in for dinner. Stop your story right now, Ruby. We'll listen while we have dinner and then I'll decide if you get dessert.'

Ruby recalled the earlier incident, when her mother was looking for her, calling out. It seemed so insignificant now. Wait until she told them about the moths, and how Bobby had rescued two of them, then surely she would get dessert.

Francis picked her up and she wrapped herself around the front of him, her arms around his neck and her legs wrapped around his waist. They looked at each other and laughed together.

Ruby's mum put on her cranky voice. 'Clean up, both of you, or else there'll be no dinner for either of you.'

Steam rose from the hot water as Ruby bathed, only her head above the water as she lay back in the old clawfoot bath. She loved the bathtub. It was deep enough for her to float in, and the warm water closed in over her, softening the mud and mulberry stains. Her dad would be in the outside shower now, scrubbing hard, removing the dried concrete and dust, the remnants of a day of hard work. She knew he would wait until she had run the bath water, letting her get the hot water first in case it ran out. After he finished, her mum would send him in to get Ruby moving.

She hated getting out of the tub. Instead, she always drew out her time, leaving it until the last moment to take the small scrubbing brush from the wire basket hanging on the wall. Then she would scrub as hard as she could, removing all of the dirt and stains from her hands and feet. She knew her mum would inspect her cleanliness, and if she had missed any marks, Ruby would have to use the bucket and cold water outside to finish off after dinner.

The door rattled as her dad banged on it. 'Hurry up, dinner's out.'

Ruby emerged scrubbed and refreshed. Her dad hugged her, one hand ruffling her hair, both revelling in the freshness of feeling clean.

The three of them sat around the small dining-room table and ate their evening meal, her mum smiling and relaxed now, her dad talking about his day. It was the usual steak and mash, carrots, and of course the greens —beans and peas. This was their favourite time of the day. It was quiet, just the family, all tucked up together, ready to chat and catch up with what each other had done during the day.

Her dad beamed at both of them. 'Righto, Ruby Rose, now tell us what exciting things you did today.'

***